INSPIRED BY THE
NETFLIX ORIGINAL SERIES

LOST
IN
SPACE®

Cover design by Christina Quintero and Elaine Lopez-Levine

Little, Brown and Company
Hachette Book Group
1290 Avenue of the Americas, New York, NY 10104
Visit us at LBYR.com

First Edition: November 2019

Little, Brown and Company is a division of Hachette Book Group, Inc.
The Little, Brown name and logo are trademarks of Hachette Book Group, Inc.

The publisher is not responsible for websites (or their content)
that are not owned by the publisher.

Library of Congress Cataloging-in-Publication Data
Names: Emerson, Kevin, author.
Title: Return to yesterday / Kevin Emerson.
Other titles: Lost in space (Television program : 2018)
Description: First edition. | New York ; Boston : Little, Brown and Company,
  2019. | Audience: Ages 8-12 | Summary: "Will Robinson stumbles upon a
  portal back to Earth and his past and triggers a series of events that could
  change his present and the future"——Provided by publisher.
Identifiers: LCCN 2019023868 (print) | LCCN 2019023869 (ebook) |
  ISBN 9780316425933 (hardcover) | ISBN 9780316425940 (ebook) |
  ISBN 9780316425926 (ebook)
Classification: LCC PZ7.E5853 Ret 2019 (print) | LCC PZ7.E5853 (ebook) |
  DDC [Fic]——dc23
LC record available at https://lccn.loc.gov/2019023868
LC ebook record available at https://lccn.loc.gov/2019023869

ISBNs: 978-0-316-42593-3 (paper over board); 978-0-316-42594-0 (ebook)

Printed in the United States of America

LSC-C

10 9 8 7 6 5 4 3 2

INSPIRED BY THE
NETFLIX ORIGINAL SERIES

LOST IN SPACE®

Return to Yesterday

An original novel by
Kevin Emerson

LITTLE, BROWN AND COMPANY
New York   Boston

Special thanks to
Synthesis Entertainment

Prologue

Mission Log 18
Robinson, Maureen—Commander
24th Mission of the Resolute

Good morning. It's day four since we evacuated the Resolute *and crash-landed here, though we still don't know exactly where here is. We're in another part of the galaxy as best as I can tell, though given that we can't even find Alpha Centauri or any other familiar stars in the sky, it's possible that somehow we've ended up in a different galaxy entirely.*

John, Judy, Penny, and Will, along with myself, continue to be in good health, aside from minor wounds sustained over these last few difficult days, and so far we've been able to balance fears of our predicament with action toward our continued survival and rescue.

Our Jupiter remains in stable condition. Since we escaped from the glacier, we have had no more instances of eels in the fuel tanks, and with this planet's relatively mild climate, we've been able to recharge the life support batteries during the day. Our supply levels have actually improved now that we've made contact with the other surviving Jupiters. Victor, our colonial representative, has implemented a resource-sharing program, and today John and I will be part of the team redistributing materials.

We still have had no contact with the Resolute, or I guess I should say they haven't heard from us. We know that they've been in orbit above this planet since the accident, but while they suspect that we are down here, they are unable to receive any of our transmissions or verify our survival, due to the loss of their scanning array. We tried to alert them to our presence with a light beam, but that attempt was thwarted by some particularly angry creatures that Will has taken to calling mothasaurs. I'm sure Hiroki's logs will explain all about those.

Now for the really bad news: I am still gathering data on the nature of the black hole that I've discovered near this system's star, but all evidence continues to point toward our time on this planet growing very short, very fast. I have confided this information in two other mission members: John and Hiroki. I plan to tell the rest of the colonists very soon, perhaps this evening, though I am worried about how it will affect morale. I haven't yet told my children, either....

For the moment, our plan remains the same as yesterday: We know of another downed Jupiter that reportedly has full fuel stores. If we can get that fuel, we should have just enough—assuming my calculations are right—to get the Jupiters airborne. Then we just need to figure out a way to modify them to carry more people. Apart from that, we will continue with day-to-day tasks, such as dispersing supplies and keeping up morale.

Last thing: There's been no change in the Robot. It continues to act as Will's protector and friend. It even *fought off those mothasaurs when they attacked, though to do that, it shape-shifted to its previous form, the version that attacked the Resolute, and seeing that scared the rest of the colonists. That Robot is responsible for us being here, for the deaths of twenty-seven colonists…and yet it's also the reason my family and I are alive. Some of the other colonists want it destroyed or at the very least imprisoned—if such a thing is even possible—but John and I can't forget how it saved Judy from the ice, how it saved all our lives that first night, when we were trapped on the glacier. So, for now John has convinced the colonists to allow the Robot to stay. We've seen its spaceship, and though we couldn't understand its technology, I can't help thinking of how much we could learn from it. I know it's a risk letting it stay with us, but I have to admit: I like knowing it's watching out for Will.*

Well, time to get to the day's tasks. I'll report again in twenty-four hours. Until then…wish us luck.

CHAPTER

1

My name is Will Robinson, and I'm in danger. We all are. Ever since my family crash-landed on this planet, one thing or another has been trying to kill us. Collapsing ice, erupting volcanoes, violent storms, and creatures you'd have to see to believe.

But sometimes I think the most dangerous thing to us all is...me.

You're probably wondering: How can an eleven-year-old boy be a danger to his family? Well, for me, it's easy. I'm not brave like my sister Judy, or creative like my sister Penny. I'm smart—really smart, actually—but that doesn't do me any good if I freeze up when things get hard. Also, it seems like no matter what I do, danger always finds me.

Of course, the most dangerous thing that ever found me also ended up saving us all. That would be my Robot. If it weren't for him, we wouldn't even have survived our first night here. With him around, I feel like I can be braver and more helpful than I've ever been, and I put us in a lot less danger.... Well, at least as far as my family knows.

Most of my family has no idea about what happened in the north cave. And if I'm lucky, the rest of them will never find out, because if they knew how bad things almost got, and all because of me...

Then again, what happened was partially *their* fault. The morning it all started, I was busy double-checking the circuit boards in the ship's life-support systems—just one of, like, twenty jobs that Mom had listed on the whiteboard for me—when Dad's voice suddenly came over the *Jupiter 2* comm system: "Kids, meet up in the common room. Your mother and I are going out."

Great, I thought, *another mission where we get left behind.* I slid the circuit board back into its socket in the wall compartment and turned to the Robot, who stood beside me.

"Come on," I said. "Family meeting."

He looked down at me, his smooth crystal face glowing with lights like thousands of falling stars, and then followed me as I walked down the circular corridor of the ship to the central common room. Mom and Dad were already there, zipping up their jackets.

"Where exactly are you going?" Judy appeared, a towel over her shoulder, still breathing hard from running on one of the treadmills down in the cargo bay. "And for how long?"

"All very good questions that your father should have answered in his announcement," Mom said, giving Dad that look that meant they were *mostly* on the same page.

"I just figured you'd know the details better than me," Dad said with a shrug.

"Of course she does," said Penny, not looking up from where she was sitting and writing in her journal. "Mom's the detail queen."

"I'll take that as a compliment," said Mom, smiling. "We have to help Victor disperse the collected supplies among the surviving *Jupiters*. I also need to do a manual check of each ship's fuel reserves to make sure my calculations are right."

"We should be back by nightfall," said Dad.

"I thought our primary goal was trying to establish contact with the *Resolute*," said Judy. "What's so important about the fuel stores?"

"Things have changed," said Mom, and her face fell. I glanced at Penny, who always noticed those kinds of things, and saw that her face had darkened, too.

"What's going on?" said Judy, looking between the two of them.

Mom breathed deep and put on a smile. "I promise we'll explain all the details once we're back, but right now we're wasting daylight. Everybody good with their job board?"

"Define *good*," Penny muttered.

"As in: You'll have it all done when we get back," said Dad.

"Aye-aye, captain," said Penny.

Dad grinned. "And remember to keep the perimeter fence armed while we're gone, got it?"

"Keep us posted," said Judy.

"We will." Mom started out, but paused to rub my shoulder. "Stay safe," she said, and her eyes flicked to the Robot, who stood behind me.

A minute later we heard the hum of the chariot fading into the distance.

"Well, back to work I guess," Judy said.

I went back to my circuit board tests. Our

Jupiter had been submerged in glacial water, and after that, Dad flew it through collapsing ice tunnels. We'd barely made it out, and the combination of impact and water damage had affected a bunch of systems. Almost every board had at least one burned-out connection, and I had to solder those back together and sometimes replace the wires and resistors. I didn't mind the work that much—it was a good chance to review circuit pathways and ship systems, and it was super important if we ever wanted to get back to the *Resolute*—but it was a little boring. Mom and Dad, even Judy, were always getting to go out on real missions and adventures, while I pretty much always got stuck here where it was *safe*.

That said, by noon I had finally finished all my jobs, so the Robot and I headed to the cockpit, where Judy was working on recalibrating the *Jupiter*'s navigation system. "We're gonna go for a hike," I said, slinging my backpack over my shoulder.

"Did you finish all your jobs?" You could always count on Judy to have memorized not only every item that Mom had left her to do, but the rest of us, too.

"Yup."

Judy looked from me to the Robot, who was right behind me. It was a look just like Mom's: the mistrust, always there no matter how many times he proved he was a friend.

"We'll be fine," I added.

Judy's lips pursed, but she nodded. "Don't be gone long. And stay inside the perimeter."

I just gave her a look.

She rolled her eyes. "Fine, but definitely stay in comm range, okay?"

"Got it." I headed for the hatch and jogged down the ramp, the Robot's footsteps thudding behind me. When I reached ground, I could feel the eyes of the other colonists nearby: all gazing at the Robot even more warily than Judy had. Some of them even looked afraid.

"It's okay," I said to him.

He didn't respond—he never did. In fact, there were only three words he ever said, and when he did, we were in trouble. But those lights in his face…they made all these different patterns and shapes, and I could just tell he was thinking so much. Sometimes I even felt like I could under-stand him. Like right then, as we stood there outside the ship, his lights were making a sort of figure-eight pattern that I always thought of as his *unsure* face.

"They're going to come around," I said, glanc-ing at the colonists, who had mostly gotten back to their duties. "You'll see."

I should probably explain why everyone was looking at the Robot this way. See, ever since I'd found him, he'd been good, with calm blue lights and a human shape, but when I first met him, he was bad. His face lights were a fire red, and he had a totally different form with multiple legs and blades for hands. That's how the colonists remembered him from when he attacked the *Resolute*.

That's also how he'd looked when I ran into him in the forest, but he'd been badly injured, and after I helped him, he did whatever I said, and he was always by my side, right there when I needed him. Kinda like having a dog, except, like, a super-strong-technologically-advanced-alien dog. And hey, no allergies!

Seriously, though, no one had ever truly been there like that for me. Judy and Penny hung out with me when they could, but they were really busy with their own lives. Mom tried to find time, too, but she was always so busy with her work on the *Resolute* mission, and before this trip, Dad was always gone. Friends? I'd had a couple, but it was never that easy. I'd always had the right answer in school, but around other kids, just hanging out, I felt like I never did. And kids notice that—when it's hard—and they're not always nice about it.

With the Robot, it was so different: It was like he got everything I said. And he would *never* hurt me or anyone I knew. I was sure of that.

But the rest of the colonists weren't. They remembered what he was. What he did.

Put all that together, and we had more fun when we were off on our own.

"Want to go check out some more of the cave system?" I asked him as we started off on our hike. His lights morphed, the figure eight changing to a simple pattern where all the stars fell toward the center. "Good. Let's go."

We left camp and headed downhill into the woods. Just after the ship was out of sight, we came to one of the little light posts stuck in the ground that marked the perimeter fence. Seeing them always reminded me of home—sorry, of Earth. (Mom said not to call it *home* anymore.) In the year before we left, we'd had to put this same kind of electric barrier around our house. Here, it was meant to protect us from the weird creatures that lived in this planet's forests, only some of which we'd actually seen. Back home, it was to protect us from other people. In some ways, this place felt safer than Earth did.

I tapped the communicator on my wrist to bring up the fence controls and momentarily deactivated the section in front of us. Then I pulled up the map I'd made of the area.

"We'll take the usual route toward the caves," I said to the Robot.

The path began by dropping down a long hill to the shore of a nearby lake. We wound along the water's edge, and soon we passed through the grove of clapping flowers. That's not their official name, just what I called them—although, since we were the first humans or intelligent beings of any kind to ever come to this planet (as far as we knew anyway) maybe that did get to be their real name. Right then they didn't look like flowers, but more like green arrows pointing straight up to about knee height. But when I walked to the middle of the grove and smacked my hands together, the buds around my feet burst open in huge magenta blooms. The Robot did the same, and the heavy thud of his metal hands made the entire grove ripple with color.

"Good one," I said.

We continued on, and the trail turned away from the lakeside and wound its way deeper into the forest. Without the lapping of the water against the shore, the forest was eerie and quiet. A cool breeze blew on our faces from the glaciers high above.

"I was thinking we could check out the caves to the south this time," I said to the Robot. He went wherever I went, but I figured he'd want to be in on the plan. "From the map, they look even bigger than the one we spent the night in. See?" I switched maps on my communicator to the harmonic frequency scan I'd made of the mountainside last time we were here.

His lights seemed to flow to the center a little faster. "Glad you agree," I said.

We walked on, weaving through the forest. The shadows were cool and dark around us, and the trees kind of looked like the pine trees that you would have seen in some of the mountain forests on Earth, at least before the Christmas Star impact that changed everything. Judy said she remembered hiking in forests like this. I think I might have, once or twice? But by the time we'd left, most of the forests anywhere near where we lived had died out completely.

Here, in the dim light, there were strange plants with iridescent leaves and also these tall, mushroom-like things. Now and then, a big, fluttery moth would bob past me, its jewel-colored wings glimmering. I always paused to watch that species, and yet at the same time, the sight of them caused a flash of adrenaline to course through me, because I knew what liked to eat them.

We reached the log bridge that crossed over a narrow crevasse. The cave system was close, a little ways past Penny's favorite waterfall, where the land started to climb steeply toward the jagged mountains.

I had just put my foot carefully up onto the log, clenching my stomach at the view of rushing water in the shadows far below, when the Robot's hand gripped my shoulder. Remember how I said there were only three words he ever said, and they were bad news?

Well, he said them:

"Danger, Will Robinson."

CHAPTER

2

I froze, pulling my foot back from the log and scanning the forest around us. It was still quiet, except for my breathing and the hum of the Robot's systems.

Then I heard a crunch. And another. Footsteps. Big, heavy ones. I leaned back against the Robot. He was looking off to the right, so I peered in that direction. More crunches in a rapid, steady rhythm. Like running.

"Is it a mothasaur?" I whispered. We'd crossed paths with them before out this way.

The Robot didn't answer. His lights had gone almost completely still, like they were hovering.

The footsteps pounded and the ground began to quake. Now I heard branches snapping, roots tearing—it sounded like this thing was in a hurry.

"Should we run?" I asked, but the Robot stayed still.

A blur of movement in the corner of my eye. The big creature burst out of the bushes on the far side of the crevasse. Its body was armor-plated and it looked like a cross between an old Earth rhino and a stegosaurus. It was running at a heavy gallop, trampling everything in its path. A second creature broke through behind it.

The Robot's fingers flexed, and his whole body seemed to tense.

"No," I said, even though my heart was pounding. "Remember, we don't hurt them if we don't have to. Got it?" They mainly fed on those moths—and plants, too, I think—but they didn't seem to mind the idea of making us into a meal when we got in their way.

The Robot made a whooshing sound kind of like a sigh.

"They're not very interested in us anyway."

The mothasaurs charged right by, parallel to the crevasse. The one in the lead tilted its big head toward us for a second, but it seemed like it was more concerned with where it was going....

Or what it was running from.

"Hey," I said, pointing to the second creature. "I think it's injured." There was a long gash along its back flank, oozing purple blood.

"Danger," the Robot repeated.

The creatures thundered past and disappeared into the brush. As their noise faded I turned to the Robot. He was still gazing in the direction they'd come from. His lights had changed to the figure-eight pattern. "You're not talking about them, are you? The danger is from something else."

The forest grew silent again. I tapped my communicator and refreshed my scan of the area.

"What's that?" A new bright dot had appeared to the north. A white blinking light that I'd never seen before. I held my communicator out for the Robot to see. "There's something up there, emitting a ton of energy.... It's right by that north section of caves." We hadn't explored there yet, either, but from my scans, those caves had looked less expansive than the ones to the south. I tapped the flashing dot and cycled through different frequency filters to analyze the source, but the results were the same each time: COMPOSITION UNKNOWN.

"Could it be a piece of your ship? Or maybe it's another part of the *Resolute*," I said. "We should probably investigate."

I stepped back onto the log bridge—

The Robot's hand gripped my shoulder again. "Danger."

"Yeah, I know there's danger." I felt a flash of frustration. Sometimes, the Robot could be worse than Mom with trying to protect me. When those eels had been eating our fuel supply, he'd even locked me in a supply closet. I knew he'd been trying his best to keep me safe, but I was stuck in there for hours. "If that's a part of one of our ships, it could be important. We're right here, and everyone else is busy."

I checked the scan again. Whatever this thing was, it was giving off a massive amount of energy. "Trust me, okay? But keep your sensors peeled. If it really is dangerous, we'll take off. Deal?"

The Robot's lights made a spiraling pattern like he wasn't happy, but he moved his hand off my shoulder.

I crossed the log bridge, holding my arms out to either side for balance. The Robot waited until I was on the other side to cross himself. We pushed through the heavy underbrush, following the mothasaurs' path of trampled leaves and broken branches. As the ground became more uneven and the trail steeper, I started to see the shadows of the mountains through the trees.

We emerged from the forest briefly and crossed a shallow area of the stream. The water was still swirling with mud from where the mothasaurs had run through it, and there was a large, cascading waterfall to our left. The caves were close now.

We ducked back into the shadows and traveled a little farther, until we finally reached the spot where the forest met a high wall of crumbling rock. Between the edge of the trees and that cliff, there was a flat, smooth area of ground with a long rectangular pit. The pit ran parallel to the cliff and had straight sides and square corners, as if someone had dug it. From my current position, it was deep enough that I couldn't see the bottom.

On the other side of the pit, I spotted a jagged triangular hole in the wall; it looked like an entrance to the north section of the cave complex.

Suddenly, my communicator started to beep and flash with a warning: RADIATION SOURCE DETECTED.

"I think whatever's giving off the signal is in there," I said, pointing to the pit. I stepped out of the bushes, but the Robot didn't move. "Come on. It won't kill us to take a quick look."

I moved carefully to the edge of the pit. It was even deeper than I expected. Like, if I fell in, it would be way over my head. Deep enough that there was a shadow over the bottom, but that couldn't dim the brilliant white light that was shining down there, so bright that I had to shield my eyes.

"Whoa. Do you see this?"

The Robot joined me at the edge.

At first it seemed like the whole floor of the pit

was glowing, but as my eyes adjusted, I saw that the light was really coming from long cylinders. There were six of them lying on their sides. Each one was a couple of meters long; standing straight up, one cylinder would probably be taller than the Robot. The cylinders had smooth metal sections at each end, and their middles were made of some clear material, like glass. I squinted and could just make out what looked like chunks of glowing mineral inside.

Another warning began to beep on my communicator: RADIATION LEVELS CRITICAL.

I opened my scanner, zoomed in on the glowing mineral, and tapped ANALYZE.

The status bar blinked and then reported: SUBSTANCE UNKNOWN.

"Are those from your ship?" But even as I asked I knew that didn't make sense. If these were parts of the Robot's crashed ship, they wouldn't be arranged neatly like this.

The Robot just gazed at the cylinders.

"Well, they're definitely not from the *Resolute*. They sort of look like batteries. Could they be fuel cells? Maybe that mineral is an energy source?"

The Robot kept looking at them.

"But fuel cells for what? And why are they lined up like that? It's like someone put them here on purpose."

My radiation sensor beeped more urgently.

"Okay, okay," I said to it. Also, I was maybe starting to feel a burning sensation on my arms and face. I stepped back from the edge of the pit so that the cylinders were out of sight. Blinking at the left-over brightness in my eyes, I peered around the pit and spotted something else.

"Check it out," I said, circling to the other side. The Robot didn't follow. "Come on." He trudged after me, looking over his shoulder as he did. "You think those mothasaurs are coming back?" He was probably right. They were easily spooked, but they were also territorial.

I crouched on the far side of the pit and ran my fingers over the ground. There were large depressions in the soil, like tracks. They were wide and rounded, almost circular, and definitely not mothasaur. And it wasn't just one set—well, unless whatever made them had a lot of legs. It looked more like a few different sets had followed the same path: The tracks made a straight line from the pit to the cave entrance.

Something crashed in the trees. Now a snorting growl.

"Danger, Will Robinson."

"Okay, okay, we'll go. Just one sec."

I slipped off my backpack and got out my video recorder and its trigger stick, then held it in front of my face and hit RECORD. "This is Will Robinson of twenty-fourth colonist group. I am"— I checked my map—"approximately three kilometers northwest of our camp, and I have just made a major discovery." I rotated the camera to take in our surroundings, and then zoomed in first on the pit, then the footprints. "It seems like someone—I don't know if we're talking human or some other life-form or what—put these containers here on purpose and then went into that cave. I mean"—I moved the camera around the clearing—"I don't see any footprints coming from anywhere else, or going anywhere.... Is it possible they came out of there? That wouldn't make any sense unless...well, unless there are beings living in the cave complex. An advanced race by the look of those cylinders. I don't see how that's possible, but—"

A mothasaur roared.

"Okay, more in a minute," I said to the camera. "First we've got to shake these creatures." I clicked it off. "Ready?" I said to the Robot.

But he had turned back toward the edge of the

clearing, and I saw that it was too late. The triangular head of one of the mothasaurs was peering out of the brush on the far side of the pit.

Another growl: The second one appeared to our right, edging toward us. To our left, the cliff wall curved and gave way to broken piles of rock slabs that would be almost impossible to climb over.

"I, um," I said, "I think they have us cornered."

CHAPTER

3

My heart pounded. I could feel myself tensing up, like my muscles were made of metal, my joints made of gears. I took a step backward. As if that was a signal, the mothasaurs stepped forward and growled louder.

The Robot looked at me, then back at the creatures. He lifted his hand and flexed his fingers, and the metallic bands around his back began to rise and move.

"No!" I said, grasping his forearm. He was changing into the version of himself that fought, the one that was *bad*. I knew he wouldn't hurt me when he was like that, but still… "We don't need that. Not yet. Remember, only if we *have* to, right?"

The Robot's bands returned to their normal position.

"Good," I said, except he looked at me like he was waiting for instructions, and I had no idea how we were going to solve our current problem. The Robot wasn't going to fight the mothasaurs, but we couldn't outrun them, and they had us boxed in. Which left that cave entrance. Would we be safe there? I took a deep breath. Had to think!

When Mom and Judy wanted to solve a problem, they made lists of pros and cons.

I glanced back at the cave entrance. Pro: It was tall, but pretty narrow. A mothasaur probably couldn't fit through it, so if we went in there, maybe we'd be out of their reach. Except, con: We'd be stuck in a cave. A cave with strange tracks leading into it...But, pro: Maybe we wouldn't have to be in there long before the mothasaurs got bored and wandered off. Only, con: What if that took until after dark, or even later? And we couldn't radio for help, because Mom and Dad were too far away, and I didn't want to bring Judy and Penny face-to-face with these things.

Another growl, another step forward.

The cave seemed like the only option that didn't immediately end in fighting or being chewed to pieces. I sized up the distance between us and the entrance. We could beat the mothasaurs there, right?

"Okay, get ready to follow me," I said.

The Robot looked at me, then back at the cave, then back at me. His lights had begun to swirl quickly.

"I know," I said. "But it's our best shot. Ready? On three." I counted down, and then spun and sprinted for the cave.

The Robot ran right beside me with his giant strides.

The mothasaurs screeched, their hooves pounding right behind us.

Come on! I thought, pumping my legs as fast as I could. Almost there…I lunged and stumbled into the mouth of the cave, plunging into darkness. The Robot twisted sideways to fit through, his back scraping on the rock. He was barely inside when the first mothasaur's snout came snapping through. As it shoved its way into the entrance, I saw that I might be wrong, that if the mothasaur wanted to, it probably could wriggle through that opening.

I took another step back into the dark, my quick breaths making clouds in the cool cave air. This space was shaped like a tunnel, the rock walls fairly smooth, with some small stalactites hanging from the ceiling, not far above the Robot's head. If the mothasaur did come in, it might not want to follow us too far into the dark, but if we went farther into the tunnel, we'd have to go slow to be sure we didn't fall into a bottomless fissure. The mothasaur was thrashing and snorting and it had already gotten its front legs through....

The Robot looked at me again.

"Yeah," I said, "I think we might have to go with plan B...."

But just then the creature stopped advancing. It sniffed the air, its snout working, and then roared, but this sounded different. It shook its head and backed out of the entrance. Once it was outside, it snorted and twisted toward its hind leg. This was the one with the wound there. It retreated a few more steps and then ran around the pit to where the other creature was still standing. They growled at each other and then leered back at us, but they stayed where they were.

"Okay," I said, breathing hard. "See? No problem." Except my insides were twisted in a knot. I looked at the cave floor and saw those same heavy tracks leading past us and into the darkness, where the tunnel sloped gently out of sight, and I felt pretty sure that the mothasaur hadn't backed off because of us; it was scared of what had given it that wound. The same thing that had made those tracks.

I tried to peer deeper into the tunnel, but my eyes hadn't adjusted from being outside, and I still had green blobs from looking at those radioactive cylinders. That said, nothing seemed to be walking out of that dark toward us, at least not yet.

"Well, I guess now we wait them out." The two creatures had begun to pace along the far side of the pit. They didn't seem interested in coming any closer, and yet they also didn't seem interested in leaving. "They'll get hungry and go eventually, right?"

The Robot just watched them.

I tapped my communicator and tried to call the

Jupiter, but I didn't have a signal. "Must be the cave walls," I said.

I looked around the floor. Other than those tracks, the dirt was smooth and damp. There was a stick lying half inside the entrance. I edged out and bent to grab it, which made one of the mothasaurs roar, but they still kept their distance.

"Here," I said, scraping the stick on the floor. "I still need to teach you tic-tac-toe." The Robot and I had started to play once before, but we hadn't had a chance to get very far before we'd gotten interrupted.

I etched the grid in the dirt. "So, the goal is to get three in a row. I'll be Xs and you can be Os." I drew an X in the middle square. "Now it's your turn." The Robot bent and made a circle with his finger in the square to the left of mine. Then I drew an X in the square above mine. The Robot drew an O beside it, on the same side as his other one. "No," I said. "I mean, see, now I can win." I drew an

X in the bottom middle, and drew a line over the three. "You want to get three, but you also want to *stop* me from getting three."

We started again and I drew my first X in the corner and decided to let him win to see if he got it. He won in three moves.

"Okay, quick learner. Or did you let me win that first game?"

The Robot bent and erased the squares. We tied, and tied again, and tied a third time, and then I got sort of distracted and the Robot won again.

"We're going to need a harder game," I said. "How's it going out there?" I looked out of the tunnel entrance. Now that my eyes had adjusted to the dark, I had to squint. The mothasaurs were still on the other side of the trench, though one had lain down. "Maybe they'll nap or something." I felt my stomach rumble. "I'm gonna have a snack."

I twisted to reach my backpack—

Something caught my eye from farther down the tunnel. Had that been movement? No...but there was a light. It was faint and pale green, and for a moment I thought it was just my eyes making stuff up.

But no, it was really there: an eerie greenish glow coming from somewhere out of sight.

"Hey," I said, tapping the Robot's arm. "Do you see that?"

His head swiveled and cocked to the side. For a moment, his processors hummed. "Danger."

"Yeah, what else is new?" I said in a half whisper.

What could possibly be down there *making* light?

And now I thought I heard something: a faint whir...but steady, almost like a machine. It might have just been a trick, like that time back on Earth when Mom had told us to listen inside this giant seashell so that we could hear the ocean.

The green light flickered a little. There was a slight hitch in that whirring sound.

This wasn't a trick. There was something down there.

I took a step forward without even realizing it. The Robot held his hand in front of me. I knew I should probably listen to him, but at the same time… "Come on," I said. "It's like with those battery things outside. It's our duty to check this out." I knew I sounded braver than I felt, that really, there was no way I would have walked farther into that cave without a giant, super-powerful robot at my side….But hey, why *have* a Robot friend if you're not going to be a little braver?

But the Robot stayed where he was and pointed with the stick to our tic-tac-toe game.

"We can play again in a minute. I promise. We'll just go close enough so we can see whatever is making that light. Get a scan and come back up."

The Robot lowered his hand, his lights back to

making their spiral, like he thought this was a bad idea.

I wonder now if he knew what was coming, if he had some idea of what we'd find. And what was *I* thinking we'd find as I started down that tunnel? To be honest, I had no idea: maybe a crashed *Jupiter*? Or maybe it had crossed my mind that we might find something from somewhere...else. After all, we'd ended up on this planet. Maybe the source of those battery things and those footprints had traveled here, too.

It's funny to think about because in a way, I was exactly right.

And yet in every other way, I was dead wrong.

CHAPTER

4

We moved deeper into the tunnel, me walking as quietly as I could, the Robot right behind me. After only a couple of meters, it got so dark I could barely see my feet. There was only the bluish glow of the Robot's lights, and whatever that green light was from up ahead. I had a headlamp in my backpack, but I didn't want to call any more attention to us, in case there really was someone or something down here.

Besides, after another few steps, the green light had gotten bright enough that I could make out the tunnel walls and floor. The air was getting cooler, too. It felt damp on my face, although some of that was the sweat beading on my forehead. I tried to breathe slowly, to stay calm. This was no time to panic and freeze up. *Relax*, I told myself, *this is the right thing to do, and you've got a super-strong robot.*

After a few more steps, the green light had gotten so bright that we were casting shadows. At the same time, it had gotten completely dark above us, and I could no longer see the ceiling. The walls were widening, too, and the slope of the tunnel was getting steeper. I started shuffling my feet in smaller steps to keep my balance.

Up ahead there was a pool of light, like this tunnel was going to open up to a wider space. I held out my hand. "Wait here," I whispered to the Robot, and then I crept ahead the last few meters, leaned against the cool rock wall, and peered around the edge.

There was a rectangular cave with a sloping

floor. It was maybe twice as wide as the common room on the *Jupiter*, but then the ceiling was a lot higher. And the walls were different than the tunnel; in here they were straight and smooth, almost like they were made of metal. I knew there were volcanic rocks that cooled into smooth surfaces like this, so maybe this was a lava tube, except the walls seemed too straight, the corners too perfect, like they had been built.

But what really mattered was the large object standing right in the middle of the room. It looked like a doorway, its edges glowing with that green light. Except *doorway* didn't seem right, because there wasn't a door. I squinted, trying to understand what I was seeing. There was a rectangular shape, like a doorframe, except with no walls on either side of it. And then, where there should have been an actual door, there was...nothing. Well, not exactly, because I couldn't see the other side of the cave through it. Instead, it was like I was looking into pure darkness, and when I squinted I saw tiny dots of light. Almost like I was looking into space.

The room seemed to be empty. As I turned back to the Robot, I saw marks on the wall right beside the tunnel: a vertical row of perfect squares, and inside each one was a grid of symbols, with intersecting lines and circles. They reminded me of hieroglyphs, except these were incredibly fine and accurate, like they'd been carved with a laser. I looked from the doorway to these symbols; if you came *from* there, you'd see these as you walked up the cave.... Maybe they were instructions.

"Come on," I whispered to the Robot, and started toward the door. My heart was pounding. What was this thing? And how could it possibly be down here?

I got out my camera and continued recording. "Okay, I'm back," I said. "We went into that cave to hide, and now we're deep inside a tunnel and we've found some kind of structure." I panned the camera around, taking in the doorway and the rest of the cave.

My boot crunched on something. I looked down and saw broken shards on the ground that were covered in dust. "The floor has some weird composition," I said. "Could be sediment, except it crunches like glass. Maybe volcanic."

I kept going and stopped in front of the doorway. The structure was composed of some kind of silver metal, and the green light was coming from thin, clear tubes. It was pulsing through these tubes almost like it was made of some kind of liquid energy. The frame ended right at the ground, but didn't seem to actually touch it. "This doorway appears to be floating," I said for my video, moving the camera slowly up and down to take in the whole thing. "I've never seen metal or circuitry like this."

But that was nothing compared to the center

of the doorway. "It's like a window out into deep space," I said. Not only were there millions of stars, there were fuzzy spots like galaxies, faint purple-and-green smudges like nebulas. I leaned forward and angled the camera. "You can see above it, and below it, and whoa—" A wave of dizziness washed over me. "It feels like you could fall right through this thing. Like, fall forever." I stepped back from it, chills running through me.

"Okay, more in a sec." I put away the camera and turned to the Robot. "What do you think it is?"

He just gazed at it, his lights now flowing out from the center in a way I hadn't seen before. Maybe it was as mysterious to him as it was to me.

I reached out and ran my finger over the metal of the doorframe. I thought it would be cold to the touch—the air was definitely cool in here—but it was warm. Not hot, just warm. I leaned a little to the left to do this, and I saw out of the corner of my eye that the view through the doorway had flattened a little, and that there was some kind of surface there. I carefully touched it with my fingers. The surface rippled like water.

And then it started to change.

"Whoa," I whispered.

The stars blurred, almost like they were stretching. Everything swirled and moved, faster and faster, like we were traveling through space. Lines began to appear, crisscrosses and arcs like those on a holographic map, and blocks of symbols like the ones by the tunnel flashed. A galaxy blurred by, now another, and then we were speeding toward what looked like the Milky Way, and then into it, past stars of all different sizes and colors. The map lines were spreading apart and then zooming in and then spreading again, like the scale kept changing, and the stars got more distant, farther apart, and then there was only one star...and then planets...and then:

Everything stopped. The view through the doorway froze.

"What?" My mouth dropped open. I stared, blinking, trying to understand what I was seeing.

A desk, a loft bed, a window with hazy amber sky outside. Posters on the walls, piles of clothes on the floor, a mess of gadgets and memory cards scattered across the desk. It was the one spot in the universe that I knew better than absolutely anywhere else.

"That's my room," I said. I looked at the Robot. He still had that spiral pattern in his lights. "Where I used to live," I added. "The planet Earth. That's where I slept, where I did my homework and made videos for my live channel...."

My throat got tight and my eyes welled up. Most of the time, I tried not to think about our old home. I remembered standing in my doorway the last time I'd ever been there, Mom hugging me, then watching out the shuttle's back window for one last glimpse as it pulled away. But it had been so long since then. And, besides, by the time that final day had come, my room had been all packed up—just bare walls and bare furniture.

But this: This was exactly how it had really looked when I'd lived in it. And the sight was almost too much to handle. Especially after all that had happened since we left.

"Sorry," I said, wiping my eyes. "It's just...How is this possible? I mean, okay, this doorway must have read my mind somehow, right? Maybe when I touched it? But I wasn't thinking about my room. So why is it showing this?"

Suddenly, the door to my room, the one *in* my house on Earth, burst open, and I came running in. The old me, from back then. "That's me!" I gasped, but then I panicked....Would I *hear* me?

But *that* me didn't seem to hear *this* me at all, or notice a space doorway in his room. "Be right out!" he—I mean, I—shouted. He held up my old video recorder. "Did you guys hear that? This is amazing. My dad is going to be home in less than an hour! Let's see what Captain Quasar thinks about that!" He turned the camera toward my desk and aimed it at an action figure that was standing next to the lamp: a man in an old-time silver space suit. The other me moved his fingers on the screen, zooming in and out on the figure's face.

"I'm talking to an old toy I had," I admitted to the Robot. "I'd had him since I was little. Dad gave him to me and I guess he was, like, a collectible, but I used to include him in my videos for comedy. Like, I'd ask him a question or say that we were going to ask his opinion, and then zoom in, and the joke was that he never responded but just always had the same face—I mean, duh, because he was plastic—but it was just a thing my viewers thought was funny." I turned to the Robot. "It was sort of like talking to you. Not that you're here for comedy...Well, you know what I mean. I wanted to bring him with me, but I lost him while I was packing." I felt my throat getting tight again.

But at the same time, watching this other me walk over to my old desk and rummage through the stuff there, it fully dawned on me: "This is my past," I said, "isn't it? This doorway is showing me a memory." The Robot looked at me. "Except that's not quite right, because if it was a memory, we'd be seeing it the way I saw it. Like, through my eyes…"

"I'm coming!" the past version of me called over his shoulder.

"I remember this," I said to the Robot. "This was, like, a month before we left for the *Resolute*, and Dad was finally coming home from his last deployment. He was gone a lot—well, really almost all the time—I don't think I'd seen him in over a year." I pointed at the doorway. "But this was the day he finally came back, and after that he was actually around. I mean, we were super busy getting ready to go, but we felt like a real family for the first time."

I remembered thinking, back then, that of all the things that sounded cool about the new life we were headed for on Alpha Centauri, the fact that I was finally going to have a dad around, for *real*, might have been the best part. I didn't totally want to leave home, but if we hadn't gone, I don't know if we ever would have gotten him back.

I laughed to myself. "He ended up being a couple of hours late because his flight was delayed. We sat around waiting and waiting, saving dinner for him. And then once he finally got there, it was actually kind of awkward, I mean, after the first hugs. We hadn't sat around the table as a family in so long, and Mom and Dad had some little disagreements. Things weren't quite normal yet, but we still laughed a lot and filled Dad in on lots of stories and...Man, it was, like, the best night."

The past version of me was still rummaging around on my old desk. *I'm getting another memory card*, I remembered, and the past me did just that and then ran out, his feet skidding on the floor because I'd only been wearing socks. Man, when was the last time I hadn't had to wear boots? Even just hanging out on the *Jupiter*, Mom insisted we always keep them on *just in case*.

Now my room was quiet again.

"It's almost, like, what if this is really..." I reached toward the doorway again. As my fingertips touched that surface, I felt a cool sensation, only this time, I kept pushing gently, and my hand started to slide through it, and then my fingers were on the other side. They were a slightly different color, too, like they would have been in that amber afternoon light, like my fingers really were back on Earth.

"Is this thing an actual doorway to my old room?" I wiggled my fingers. "Like a portal through space-time, maybe an Einstein-Rosen bridge, you know, a wormhole, which should be impossible with any human technology, but still... Do you think I could *go* there?"

My old room. That afternoon...

I was stepping closer without even thinking about it, my hand sinking up to the wrist, my whole hand in the past, in my old room, my home—

The Robot gripped my shoulder firmly, stopping me.

"Danger." He pulled gently, like he was trying to say, *Don't go.*

I almost shook free and went anyway. To be there again...

But I pulled my hand back. "You're right," I said. Besides, I had no idea what would happen if I really went through. As soon as my fingers lost contact with the surface of the doorway, that view of my old room vanished. The surface rippled and it winked back into a field of stars and galaxies. A pit opened up in my stomach. I nearly reached out and activated it again.

"But we definitely need to investigate this thing further," I said, starting back toward the tunnel. "Technology like this...What if it's a way for us to get off this planet? For you, too? We should go back and tell Mom and Dad. They won't believe it!"

I noticed I wasn't hearing footsteps and I turned back to see the Robot still gazing at the doorway. "Coming?" I said.

He stared at it for another second before he turned and followed me. Sometimes I really wished he could say what he was thinking.

We hiked back up the tunnel, and when we got to the entrance, we saw that the mothasaurs had left. "Let's hurry," I said. "They'll probably be back as soon as they smell us."

As we jogged across the clearing and into the

bushes, I glanced at those strange glowing battery things. We still had no idea who or what was responsible for those....

But the whole way back to camp, all I could think about was that view of my room, my old life. And even though it was many months and millions of light-years in my past, suddenly it felt like I'd just left yesterday. I wanted to go back there again so badly, except if I'm being honest, it was more than that: I *had* to.

CHAPTER

5

"Mom? Dad?"

No answer. Of course, they said they'd be gone awhile, but I checked the bridge and the supply rooms anyway, and continued down the curved hallway, looking into each room.

"Penny? Judy?"

No reply from them, either, but then I found Penny standing in the common room.

"Hey!" I said, but she had her back to me and her earbuds in. She twirled around on her toe, her eyes closed, threw out her arm, and sang.

"*Tomorrow you'll be worlds away, and yet with you, my world has started…*" She spun in my direction and opened her eyes. "Ah! Why are you spying on me? Get out of here!"

"I'm not spying! I was just looking for everybody."

Penny tapped at her communicator and then pulled out her earbuds, her face beet red. "Well, next time maybe knock or something."

"The doors were open. What were you listening to?"

Penny rolled her eyes. "Just one of the very best novels-and-then-musicals ever written. I suppose I'll be the only one who remembers it where we're going."

"I remember you singing that, around the house," I said. "It was the musical you did the summer before we left, right? You were really good. I mean, as far as I could tell."

"Thanks. I *was* good." Penny sighed. "For whatever that's worth now."

"Have Mom and Dad checked in yet?"

"They called and said they're going to be delayed. What else is new? Probably not back until nightfall. Maybe even the morning. Why, what's up?"

I bit my lip. "Um…we kinda found something out at the caves. Something amazing."

"Like what?"

"It's hard to explain. I mean, I don't even know if I *can* explain it. Maybe Mom could."

"Sounds spooky. And way more interesting than this list Mom left me to do." Penny's eyes lit up. "Wanna show me instead?"

"Show you what?" Judy appeared in the doorway.

"Will found something creepy out at the caves," said Penny. "He's going to take me out there."

"I didn't say it was creepy.…"

Judy frowned. "What about your list?" she said to Penny. "There's no way you're done."

"Okay, *Mom*, no, I'm not, but I'm also about to

die of boredom. Besides, why does young William get to go off tromping through the woods all day?"

Judy crossed her arms. "Because he finished his list."

"*Because he finished his list,*" Penny mocked. "Come on, that's because Mom gives him the easy jobs, not to mention he has a super-strength helper!"

"Rehabbing circuit boards is *not* that easy," I said. "Also, I had to calculate thermal load limits on all six of the heat shield units for this specific atmosphere. *You* try that."

"Okay, let's all settle down," said Judy. "Will— hey." Her eyes narrowed and she reached toward my face.

"What?"

"What happened here?" She touched my cheek and I flinched. The skin felt hot there.

"I don't know, what do you mean?"

"It looks like a burn. There's even a little blistering, but the sun's not that strong today...." Judy moved her finger to my neck, and I winced at a stinging feeling. "Are these radiation burns?"

"I don't know," I said, and yet, I remembered my communicator's warnings. "Maybe?"

"Will." Judy was using her full Mom tone now. "What exactly did you find out there?"

"Well, I think maybe we found something... alien."

"Like him?" Penny said, pointing to the Robot.

"No, this is different."

"You mean different aliens?"

"I don't know, exactly. It's easier to show you, but it might be sort of, like, a time machine or something? Maybe an Einstein-Rosen generator?"

"Both of those things are impossible," Judy said immediately.

"Yeah, but so was he," I said, pointing to the Robot, "until we found him."

Judy kept looking at my cheek. "Push up your sleeves."

"Why?"

"Do it. Doctor's orders."

I did, and was surprised to see red streaks on both my forearms.

"Where exactly is this thing you found?" Judy asked.

"It's in a cave, north of those ones where we spent the night that time. And there are these battery things and footprints and..."

"And what?" said Judy.

Just thinking of it made my throat tight again. "I saw my old room. Our old house."

Penny squinted at me. "Did you also bump your head or something?" She motioned to Judy. "You should check his head."

"I'm fine."

Penny snapped her fingers. "I heard about these mushrooms once where just stepping on them could make you hallucinate. There could be something like that on this planet, especially in a cave—"

"I'm not making this up, Penny! I really saw it!"

"Saw it how?" said Judy.

"Through this machine." I got out my camera. "Look." I played my most recent video. "It's kinda hard to see, but it's there." Both of them leaned forward, squinting at the dark picture.

"What is that thing?" said Penny.

"It's like a doorway." The video ended. "And when I touched it, it showed me our house from, like, a month before we left. And I think... I think if you went through it, you would *be* there."

"Be where?" Penny asked. "You mean on Earth?"

I shrugged. "I know that sounds impossible, but..."

"You have to take us there." Penny's face had suddenly gotten even more serious than Judy's. "It could be a way off this planet."

"Okay, hold on. Obviously you found something weird," said Judy. "But there's no way that some door in a cave is going to get us off this planet. Besides, there's clearly significant danger of radiation exposure. At the very least, we should wait for Mom and Dad."

"Those burns aren't that bad—" said Penny.

"Excuse me, and you got your medical training *where*, exactly?"

Penny's eyes narrowed. "Oh, you love to bring up how special you are."

"Guys!" I shouted.

"I'm just saying," said Penny, "if there's any chance of finding a way off this planet, we need to check it out, and soon."

I peered at her. "How come you sound so serious? Do you know something we don't?"

Penny looked away. "I just know that we should check it out."

"I have no idea if it really can get us off this planet, but I think you'll like seeing our old home. And also"—I turned to Judy—"these burns are *why* we should go now. Once Mom sees them, she'll probably never let us near it again. It's not that far."

Neither one of them responded for a moment.

"You're right about Mom," Judy said quietly. "And I'm done with *my* list."

"Oh my god, seriously?" said Penny.

"Okay…" Judy stepped to the central table and picked up Penny's whiteboard. "How about we make a deal: We work together to finish Penny's jobs, and then you show us."

"You're serious?" I said.

Judy nodded. "Whatever technology you found, we'll be saving Mom and Dad time by doing some recon on our own. And I know you guys think I'm, like, all business, but I miss home, too, kind of all the time."

I grinned. "Thanks, Jude."

She ran her finger down the list. "Will, you and the Robot do the ration reorganizing. Mom wants the packets arranged by food group rather than alphabetical. I'll take air filter changes, and we'll meet outside when we're done. Cool?"

"Deal," said Penny.

I led the Robot out of the common room. On the way to the galley, I stopped at the gear locker and gathered two lengths of safety line and a climbing harness and stuffed them into my backpack. "Just in case we decide it is a good idea to go through that doorway," I said to the Robot, the vision of my room still right there in my mind.

It only took ten minutes to reorganize the food packets, which seemed like kind of a silly job considering that all the freeze-dried foods basically tasted the same, and then we waited outside for Penny and Judy.

Soon we were on our way back to the caves,

following the trail along the lake and then through the woods.

"We have to watch out for the mothasaurs," I said after we crossed the log bridge and neared the clearing, but when we arrived, they were nowhere to be seen.

Judy stepped cautiously toward the pit and peered inside. "These are the source of the radiation?"

"Yeah, I thought they might be batteries or something."

"They do look sorta like energy cells." Judy removed a short, silver wand-like device from her bag and waved it over the pit, then checked the readings on the thin screen on its side. "It's an unknown radiation signature, but it's strong."

"My scanner didn't recognize it, either."

"That should be impossible," said Judy. "Unless this is made of some radioactive element that has never been discovered on Earth or Alpha Centauri."

"The universe is a big place," said Penny.

Judy just pursed her lips, then she pointed at the batteries. "These were clearly arranged this way on purpose. Look, there's a coating of dust on the first three, but then these two are a lot cleaner, like they were brought here more recently. Maybe whoever places them only comes once in a while."

"But comes from where?" said Penny. "Out of that cave? Or…" She looked toward the sky.

"The tracks go to and from the cave," I said. "They might use the doorway."

"And what if they decide to use it while we're down there?" said Judy.

I shrugged. "They weren't there before. And, like you said, if they only come here once in a while, and they were just here, then we should be okay."

Judy crossed her arms and looked from the cave to the pit. I was sure she was about to call this off…. "Lead the way," she said.

They followed me around the pit and into the cave entrance.

"Whoa—check it out," Penny said in a whisper. "Alien tic-tac-toe."

"That was me and the Robot," I said.

"Still alien."

We walked on and the darkness closed in around us, the air growing cool as the tunnel descended.

"I can't see a thing," said Penny.

"Your eyes will adjust," I said. I was just starting to make out the greenish glow from up ahead.

There was a scuffling sound. "Ow!" Penny hissed. "Can't we use a light?"

"You won't need one in a second," I said. "Just a little farther."

We walked in a close line down the sloping tunnel and reached the cave. Seeing it again, with its smooth, almost-straight walls, it felt more accurate to call it a room.

"Whoa," said Penny, heading straight for the doorway. "Are those stars?"

"And galaxies."

She peered through it at different angles. "How is that possible?"

"Did you guys see this?" Judy had crouched and was running her gloved finger over those sharp patterns on the floor that I'd noticed before. She pinched a piece and picked it up, and then blew on it. A layer of dust came free, revealing a triangular transparent object. It had jagged edges, as if it had been broken.

"It almost looks like a circuit board," I said.

"Yeah, except look at the materials and surfaces." She came over and held it up beside the doorway.

"It's really different than this doorway," she said, "and both of them are different than anything human-made."

"So what?" said Penny. "Are you saying there have been two different kinds of aliens in this cave?"

"I have no idea what I'm saying," Judy said quietly.

"Well, there's nobody here *now*, so, Will, show us how this thing works."

"Okay." I stepped up to the doorway. "Oh, wait." I fished my video recorder out of my pocket, started it recording, and held it in one hand while I reached toward the doorway with the other. "I am about to officially activate the doorway," I narrated. My heart pounded and my fingers were shaking, and even though I'd been thinking about it since the second we left here, now that I was right in front of it again, I almost didn't want to touch it. But I pressed my fingers to the liquid-like surface, and the stars rippled and blurred, the view hurtling through space and time. There were the spirals of the Milky Way, huge stars flying by, then our solar system...

And my room. Just like before. Seeing it made a shock run through me all over again.

"No way," said Penny.

"That's impossible," said Judy. Both of them stared, eyes wide, mouths half-open.

"I'm glad you guys can see it, too," I said. "I was wondering if maybe I'd been losing my mind."

"If you are, then we are, too," said Penny.

"Now, just watch." We waited a moment, and the old me came into the room, calling over his shoulder.

"Whoa, you look younger," said Penny.

The past version of me narrated his video, found the memory card, and hurried out.

Once the room was still, I stopped my own recording and put my recorder back in my pocket. Then I reached for the doorway.

"What are you doing?" Penny asked.

"Will, don't—" said Judy.

I pushed my fingers through the energy field and flexed them in the amber light of Earth. "It's all right, see? I did this before."

"Does it feel weird?" said Penny.

"Maybe a little tingly. Not bad for reaching across the universe, right?"

"If I touched it, would it show this same thing?" Penny asked. "I mean, probably not, right? It would show me somewhere in *my* past instead."

"How can it possibly be doing this?" Judy said. "And why?"

"Maybe it's, like, a default setting," said Penny. "Like when you'd get on the *Resolute*'s network and your favorite pages would automatically load."

"So this thing is showing us a favorite memory?" said Judy.

"It's not a memory, though," I said, "not exactly. Because it's not from my point of view. And if I can put my fingers through, it must be an actual connection to that spot. But you're right, this is a favorite moment. The night Dad came home...or maybe I should call it an *important* moment. You know, to me, like—"

"Emotionally," said Penny.

"That was a fun night," Judy said quietly.

"Maybe it uses our memories like coordinates," I said, and when they both just looked at me, I said, "You know, in space-time. To guess where we might want to go."

Judy shrugged. "But to do that, this thing would have to have essentially scanned your entire brain and translated your memories, as well as the emotions connected to each one—"

"You could just say it read his mind," said Penny.

"My point is that it did all that in the second when you touched it. I mean, the processing power alone that you would need to do that…"

"So maybe those things outside really are its power cells," I said. Except there wasn't any port or outlet or anything on this doorway, and there wasn't one of those batteries connected to it now.

"I wonder what other spots it could open up to," said Penny.

"Will, you should pull your hand back," said Judy. "We don't know what effect that's going to have, and you already got those radiation burns."

"Those were from those cells outside. My fingers feel fine, see?" I moved them around.

"Okay, but what if your old self comes back and sees random fingers twiddling in space in his room? Won't that create, like, a paradox or something? And mess up the fabric of the universe?"

"Jeez, way to be a downer," said Penny.

"We have to think about this stuff!" Judy nearly shouted. "We are messing with something we literally don't understand."

"Yeah," I said quickly, "but if old me had walked in and seen fingers like that, me-of-right-now would remember it, wouldn't I?" I said. "The fact that I never remember seeing anything strange in my room is proof."

Judy nodded but she was still pursing her lips. "That makes sense... *if* that's how this kind of thing works. There's no way to be sure because no one's ever found a time doorway in a cave before."

I started taking off my backpack. "You're right, and that's part of the reason why"—I removed the safety line and the climbing harness—"I was thinking this time I should try going all the way through."

"Uh-uh," said Judy. "No way."

"Definitely yes," said Penny, her eyes lighting up. "Then we'll know if this really is, like, a way home."

"That's not home," said Judy. "That's the past. Our home is here."

"This place isn't home!" said Penny. "It totally sucks, and not only that—"

"I mean *now* is home," said Judy. "Like, the present. Going back there risks messing with physics in ways we can't understand."

"But clearly it's not dangerous," said Penny. "Will already put his hands through and nothing changed. And like he said, he doesn't remember anything strange from his past, so we're good."

"For the moment," said Judy. "But we don't know how our actions might change the past, or what even a little change could lead to."

"But that's not really possible, is it? Like, actually changing the past?" said Penny. "I thought those sci-fi ideas like bootstrap paradoxes, while awesome by the way, were impossible. Isn't the past, like, finished?"

"There are competing theories," I said, "but nobody knows for sure."

"Which means it's dangerous," said Judy. "Like, existentially dangerous."

I knew she had a point, but I bent and pulled the harness over my legs. That view, my room, it was like a magnet drawing me in. "Don't worry," I said. "I'll be super careful."

As I snapped the buckles into place, I felt my heart pounding and I wondered: Was I crazy?

Because I definitely believed in the possible dangers that Judy was describing. And yet, after all this time thinking I'd never see my room, our home, Earth, ever again, I mean, I had to go, right? At least for a minute?

"I'm just going to step through," I said, clipping the rope to my harness. "I'll come right back. And you guys will be able to see me and you'll have the line, so you can pull me back even sooner if you need to."

"But what about the you in the past?" said Judy. "What if you—I mean, he—sees you?"

"I think I have a little time," I said. "I remember that I was making a video about Dad coming home, so I should be out in the living room filming for a little bit."

"Maybe I should go," said Judy, putting her hand on my shoulder. "You're the youngest; it's not fair."

"Here she goes again," said Penny.

For a second I almost said *Okay*, just like I always

did when Judy stepped in to help. But then I pictured her in the ice—my fault. "No," I said. "It should be me. It's my room, and I found this place."

"Will—"

"We should both be here to pull him back if we need to," said Penny. She picked up the line and tugged it. "Sorry, you don't get to be the hero, Jude."

Judy's face scrunched. "That's not what I meant."

"Okay, okay," I said. "I'm going." I looked at the Robot. He was staring into the doorway, and then turned toward me. "If this is the worst idea ever, now is the time to say so." He cocked his head, and I was sure he would say *Danger*, or even hold me back—did a part of me even want him to?—but he didn't say a word.

"All right, here we go." I moved my foot toward the barrier. My toe made the surface ripple, and then it was on the other side. Now my whole foot, and I was standing half in and half out of the past and, if we were right, basically straddling the galaxy.

"Does it hurt?" said Penny.

"No," I said. "It doesn't feel like anything. Just tingly again. Okay…here we go."

I took a deep breath and put my weight on that foot, and then my hands pushed through the barrier, then my arms, and I closed my eyes and stepped through.

CHAPTER

6

There was a bright flash, and a buzz of electricity shot through me. I blinked, and for a second there were only green spots in my eyes, but as they faded, I saw that I was—

Home. Standing in my room on Earth. I felt the afternoon light through the window and the smoggy sky. I heard the hum of the air purifiers that made the whole house vibrate, and the low murmur of a TV out in the living room. The clinking of dishes. The smell of the sweet-salty noodle dish that Mom was making—Dad's favorite.

I breathed deep, and then reached out and ran my finger over the edge of my desk. It was real. I was really here!

There was a tug on the safety line.

I turned, and there was the doorway behind me. Instead of seeing my loft bed, I saw Penny and Judy standing in the cave. Penny raised her arms as if to say, *So?*

I gave them a thumbs-up and took another step, my foot pushing through my old clothes scattered all over the floor. I had this dizzy feeling, like my head were an inflated balloon. Probably because I had just literally traveled through space and time, but also because this was completely crazy!

A light flashed on my communicator. It was displaying a warning message: INCOMPATIBLE NETWORK. It must have been trying to log on, but this communicator was designed for the *Resolute's* advanced system, not the older networks we'd had on Earth. I tapped the message and swiped it away.

But then I froze as a figure passed the open door—Penny, the past version of her, wearing a bathrobe with her hair up in a towel. "Mom!" she called. "Where are all my shirts?"

"Probably still in the laundry waiting for you to put them away," I heard Mom reply.

I edged toward the door and peered out. There was Mom in the kitchen. In one hand she held a spoon poised over the steaming wok. With the other, she was swiping her finger across a tablet screen, probably going over the latest mission results. Especially in those last months before we left, it seemed like she'd been basically working all the time. We had a rotation of making dinners and doing other household chores, but I remembered that she had wanted to cook tonight because it was some recipe that she and Dad had learned while on their honeymoon.

There was Penny, returning from the utility room, the laundry cart humming along behind her.

"I see you found them," said Mom.

Penny rolled her eyes. "We can go to another star system, but we can't invent a way to fold laundry."

Mom grinned. "I'm sure we could, but it builds character."

"If your character is into suffering and toil."

"That sounds like high literature."

"Whatever. Hey!" Penny shouted. "Will!"

I actually opened my mouth before I remembered that she wasn't talking to me, and instead I leaned away from the door.

"Yeah?!" My past self appeared, recorder out in front of him. It was so weird to see myself. And that version of me had no idea that *this* me was standing right here!

"Get your robotics junk off the couch so I can fold the laundry."

"Can't you just work on the floor?" the old me asked.

"Nope."

"Ugh, come on!" The old me rolled his eyes and sighed—jeez, I looked kind of melodramatic—but then he started clearing stuff.

"What's Dad's ETA?" Penny asked as she dropped to the couch.

"Flight should finally be touching down in a half hour, then he just has the usual gridlock to contend with."

"Is Judy deigning to join us?" Penny asked.

"Yes," said Mom, "she has finals this week, but she said she'd be here."

I watched my former self finish moving my gear and then pick up my recorder. "And here we have Mom making dinner," the old me said, aiming the camera as he walked into the kitchen.

The safety line tugged again. In the cave, the girls were waving at me to come back. I raised my hands like, *Why?* but they motioned more emphatically.

I glanced back toward the living room and had to fight the urge to just step out there and be like, *Hey! It's me! From the future!* I wanted to be part of this night again so badly. And then another thought crossed my mind: I could warn them! About the *Resolute* attack, the crash...but I reminded myself about the dangers of changing the past, and instead turned back to the doorway.

I was crossing my room when Captain Quasar caught my eye. I reached over and grabbed him, which made Judy freak out and wave her hands like, *No,* but she didn't know how upset I'd been that I'd lost this thing. And given that I was going to lose it anyway, I figured that taking it right now wouldn't matter.

I moved to the doorway, gritted my teeth, and stepped through. Another buzzing, and a white flash, and then I was back in the cool and dark of the cave. I shivered and all at once it hit me that I was literally a world away from home. I looked over my shoulder, thinking, *I want to go back*, but the doorway had returned to its neutral view of stars.

"Are you all right?" Judy took my wrist and felt my pulse.

"Yeah, fine."

"Then what were you thinking, taking that thing?" She pointed to the action figure. "Didn't you hear what I said about altering the past?"

"Yeah, but it's okay! I lost this before we moved, so it won't change anything. Also, I wanted to see if I could really transport something through the door. This proves that it's not just a hallucination or something."

"Well…that is technically a good point," Judy admitted.

"Thank you." I held up the little figure for the Robot to see. "Cool, huh?"

"What was it like?" said Penny, her eyes wide. "Bigger on the inside?"

"You mean my room?"

Penny rolled her eyes. "Never mind. How was it really? You know, being back there?"

"Super weird," I said, "but also normal. You were there, doing laundry, and Mom was making dinner."

"Teriyaki soba?" said Penny, inhaling. "Some of that came back through with you." Then her nose wrinkled. "*Ooh*, and also some of the lair of stinky feet!"

"Shut up! My room didn't smell like that."

"You just didn't notice," said Judy. She was studying the side of my face.

"What?"

"Your burn looks the same. Pulse is in the normal range.... And you feel okay?"

"Yeah, a little light-headed, maybe, kind of like how I used to feel after doing the zero-g simulator... but otherwise I think I'm okay." Just as I said that, my vision prickled with spots. "Actually, I need to sit down for a sec."

The Robot turned his head toward me as I sat on the cave floor. "It's nothing," I said. "And see? No danger."

The lights in his face bloomed for a moment, almost like fireworks, and then a small light began to flicker on the metal housing to the side of his face.

"What's that?" I asked him.

The little light kept flickering.

"Okay," said Penny. "My turn." She stepped up to the doorway and held her hand out for the harness.

I slipped it off my legs and handed it to her.

"Be careful, Penny," said Judy.

"Why do you say that to *me*? It's no different than him going."

"We'll see," said Judy. "Where do you think it will open for you?"

"No idea."

"Wait!" I said. "We can test that. I mean, where it opens. For me, I didn't even know what the doorway did when I touched it, and it picked that day. It's almost like it was trying to anticipate what I wanted, the way a search engine uses predictive text."

"Like a virtual assistant," said Penny, "except for time travel."

"Right," I said, "so what if you think of a specific place you want to go *before* you touch it? That way we'll know if we can control where this thing takes us."

Penny thought for a moment. "Got it. I want to go to dress rehearsal."

"When was that?" asked Judy.

"It was, like, four months before we left, remember? *A Midsummer Night's Dream*? I was Hermia... as a *freshman*? Hello? Not like you were there."

"I had a double course load," said Judy. "Mom said you were really good in it."

"She was," I said. "I remember that." I decided not to tell her that I hadn't understood the play at all and had *maybe* fallen asleep for a little bit.

"Let's see if it works." Penny turned to the doorway and said, "Please take me to my dress rehearsal." She reached out to touch the surface.

The view of space swirled and moved and spiraled, and once again, we were shooting through the stars, the map lines and symbols flashing, finding the Milky Way, diving into our solar system...and then the doorway stopped on a view of the high school auditorium.

"It worked," I said, sharing a grin with Penny.

"Won't there be a lot of people around?" said Judy.

"Nope," said Penny. "Dress rehearsal was on a Friday morning during school. The show opened that night. Classes weren't invited, so there was almost nobody around. Perfect time for a magical doorway to appear."

We were seeing the stage from the back of the

auditorium, with all the rows of empty seats between here and there. "Did you think of having the door in the back so nobody would see it?" I asked.

"Sure did."

"So we know this thing is pretty incredibly accurate."

"Okay, I'm going." Penny tightened the harness.

"I still feel like this is pushing our luck," said Judy.

"What's the point of luck if you can't use it?" said Penny. "It's like you guys said, once Mom and Dad see this thing, the fun will be over, and I am not missing my chance."

"Penny, you have to remember," said Judy, "don't interact with yourself or change the past at all. We can't risk it."

"Yeah, yeah. We already know that I don't, same as Will, because I don't remember any weird space-traveler version of myself showing up at dress rehearsal. Besides, Will even took that little space guy and nothing changed." She tugged on the knot at her waist. "It will be fine." Her eyes were wide with excitement. "Be right back!"

She breathed deep and stepped through. The doorway rippled and then there she was, standing in the dark auditorium.

"I hope she's careful," Judy said, crossing her arms.

"Did you say that about me when I was gone?" I asked.

"I didn't have to."

I glanced back at the Robot and saw that his little strobe light was still flashing, and his face lights were almost completely still.

Penny moved through the shadows and slid into a seat in the back row. We could see her earlier self onstage, her arms moving as she spoke her lines with the others, but we couldn't quite hear what she was saying.

"Well, this is boring," said Judy.

Something caught my eye. "Someone's coming!"

"Oh crap." Judy tugged on the line.

Penny twisted to look back at us, and then noticed the figure coming toward her.

"If she gets caught," said Judy, "when she's also right there on the stage…"

Our version of Penny looked from the figure to the doorway, like she was considering jumping back through—

But then the figure stopped and faced the front of the auditorium. I could see now that it was an adult, and he held up a tablet and began moving a finger up and down on the screen.

"I think it's the light-and-sound guy," I said.

He fiddled with the settings a bit more and then walked away.

Penny looked at us and made a gesture like a huge sigh of relief.

Judy tugged the rope again. "She should come back. This is too dangerous."

But Penny didn't move right away. She kept watching the show. Judy tugged again, and this time Penny's head whipped around with an annoyed expression. She held up her finger as if to say, *One more minute,* then she got up and walked out of our view to the side of the door.

"What's she doing?" said Judy.

"Probably just taking it all in," I said.

"I have a bad feeling about this."

If I was being honest, I did, too, not that I wanted to side with one sister over the other.

Turns out, I should have. All of a sudden the line pulled tight.

"Hey!" Judy began—

And then it fell slack in her hand. "Oh no." Judy pulled and the line started to flop through the doorway way too easily. A moment later, an object flashed through and landed at our feet.

It was the harness. Empty.

CHAPTER

7

"Penny!" Judy shouted, her voice echoing in the cave.

"What's she doing?" I jumped up and tried to look through the door, but I didn't see her anywhere.

"We have to go get her," said Judy. She bent and grabbed the harness. "I'll go, and you get ready to—"

"Wait!" I put a hand on her arm. "I don't think that will work."

"Will, we can't—"

"No, listen! The doorway reacts to whoever touches it, right? So as soon as you try to go through, it might change locations to somewhere based on your thoughts."

Judy paused, but she was still gripping the harness tightly.

"And if the doorway changes locations," I continued, "Penny will be trapped where she is, and there will be no way to get it back there, because it's not our memory."

Judy bit her lip. Then she huffed and threw down the harness. "You're right. Of course you're right. Ugh, she's so irresponsible!" Judy craned her neck to see around the edges of the doorway view. "Where the heck did she go?"

"I don't know," I said. "Any ideas?" I asked the Robot. He just gazed at the doorway with that strange little light still flickering.

A minute passed, then three. I felt another wave

of light-headedness so I sat back down, crossing my legs.

"Five minutes," Judy reported, looking at her communicator.

Then it was ten.

"You know, ever since we left Earth, she's at least been a little more thoughtful about other people," Judy muttered. "Figures that the minute she gets back there, she immediately reverts to good old *Penny-the-center-of-the-universe.*"

"Yeah," I said, except I thought Judy was being kind of harsh. Sure, Penny had been wrapped up in her friends and the theater program and her writing, but she'd also played video games with me and stuff. But Judy probably hadn't seen that, because she'd been off at medical school until late every night. I wanted to say something, but I also didn't want to make things any more uncomfortable.

Then fifteen minutes had passed. Through the

door, the play went on, the old Penny moving around the stage with the other actors.

"If she went to see that boyfriend, I'll kill her," said Judy.

"Andras? She wouldn't do that. I mean, that would mess up her memories and stuff like we talked about. Plus, she broke up with him before we left."

Twenty minutes.

Judy sat down beside me, her chin in her hands.

"At least the doorway is still open to the same spot," I said. "That might be a good sign. You know, that everything's okay."

"*Mmm.*" She checked her communicator. "Okay, we cannot just sit here waiting forever. If she's not back after thirty minutes, I'm going to try going through that door."

"We still have some time," I said. I could hear that determined tone in Judy's voice, the one that could overrule her incredibly smart brain and make her do something crazy. And I didn't think I'd be able to talk her out of it.

Twenty-five minutes.

Judy threw up her hands. "Does she have any idea the kind of trouble she could cause? Is she even thinking of how worried we are?"

"She probably doesn't realize how long she's been gone," I said.

Twenty-seven minutes—

There was a blur of movement in the doorway.

"Danger," said the Robot. That light on the side of his face was still flickering.

"There she is!" said Judy, leaping to her feet.

Penny—our Penny—appeared, creeping back into our view. She was hunched over with her arms cradled in front of her, holding something. Her face was red, and her hair was messy. As she neared, she couldn't contain a huge grin on her face and a wild brightness in her eyes.

"I'm glad she's back," Judy said with a sigh, "but I don't like that look."

Penny lunged through the doorway and dropped to her knees, making a wheezing sound. Behind her, the doorway swirled back to its starscape.

"Are you all right?" I asked.

She looked up and we saw that she was laughing. "Oh man," she said, "that was insane."

"Where did you go?" Judy shouted. "What were you thinking?"

"Sorry," she said between heavy breaths. "I was busy having a genius moment." She spread her arms. "Behold!"

Packages of candy tumbled onto the cave floor. "Whoa, score!" I said. There were Star Chews, Sour Fizz, Green Tea Drops, and Cocoa Pandas. We hadn't seen candy like this since we'd left. The *Resolute* only had two desserts: rehydrated chocolate cake that basically tasted like chalk and a tan synthetic pudding that just tasted sweet. I didn't think we'd ever see this stuff again. "Is this for everybody or—"

"Nah, you kidding?" said Penny proudly. "There is no way I'm sharing this with the rest of the colonists. It's just for us! Dig in!"

I picked up the lime-green Star Chews bag, running my fingers over its smooth surface. My mouth had already started watering.

"Go ahead and tear that sucker open, Will!" said Penny.

"Wait, hold on," said Judy. "Penny, where did you get this?"

"You know, a simple *thank you, my amazing sister* would be sufficient."

Judy crossed her arms. "Where?"

Penny cocked her thumb at the doorway. "I went over to Corner Market. The place near school."

"You did *what*?"

"Relax, big sister, nobody even saw me. I didn't pass anyone I knew on the way there or back. But even if I had run into someone, they would've just thought that I was, you know, *me*. And kids always run for snacks during rehearsal."

I thought that made sense and turned my attention back to the more important topic, which was opening the Star Chews package.

"Okay," said Judy, "but how did you pay for this stuff?" She pointed at Penny and made a circle with her finger. "It's not like *this* you has a credit account that would work on Earth anymore."

When Penny didn't answer right away, I looked up and, even though it was dark in the cave, it looked like her face had gotten red.

"So...slight technicality," she admitted. "I didn't really think about that part until I was there. To be honest, I didn't think about even going to the market at first. I just wanted to get outside and breathe it in and look around. You know, *be* there. Then it occurred to me: snacks! It wasn't until I was inside the store that I thought about the *money* thing, but then it didn't matter because the counter guy stepped into the back for something, and I don't even think he'd really seen me come in, so..." She looked away.

"Wait, did you *steal* this?" Judy said, her eyes bugging.

"Well, I mean, sort of? But it wasn't even really me, right? I was still in school, so..."

"But it *was* you!" Judy's voice echoed in the cave. "If you'd been seen, if you'd gotten caught—"

"Yeah, but I didn't!" she snapped. "I'm here and everything is the same as it was. Now stop doing your mom impersonation for a minute or I'm not even going to share this with you." She picked up a package of Green Tea Drops and tore them open.

I fished out one of the sugar-dusted Star Chews.

It was dark red: pomegranate. I popped it in my mouth and my taste buds exploded at the combination of sour and sweet. Man, I'd forgotten how much I loved these!

The candy filled my mind with memories, too, ones that, since we'd arrived here, I'd barely thought about. Like walking home from school with my neighbor Ali, who was also in the after-school engineering elective, and stopping at the very same Corner Market Penny had just visited. I could picture the cluttered aisles, that stale white lighting inside. We used to get snacks and eat them on the way home, and we always sat on the rock wall near our houses to finish them because we'd been too busy talking....

"Good, right?" said Penny, smiling at me.

"Amathin'," I said around the gooey candy. Clumps of it were sticking in my teeth just the way they used to. "You'wan'wun?" I held out the package to the Robot with a candy-covered grin.

"Danger," he said.

"Fine, have it your way."

"What does he eat anyway?" said Penny.

"Battery charge," I said.

"Yeah, I know—it was a joke."

Judy huffed. She was still frowning, and gave Penny another quick glare, but then she picked up the roll of Cocoa Pandas and quietly sang, "*Cocoa Pandas in a tree.*" Hearing that old jingle made us all grin at one another. She dug into the foil top of the roll, peeled it back, took one, and then passed them around.

Penny had a mouthful of tea drops, but she took a Cocoa Panda anyway and shoved it in, too—which made her crack up, and then me.

"*Mmmm*, so good," she mumbled.

"The best!" I said, letting a Cocoa Panda melt in my mouth.

Even Judy couldn't help laughing. Now she tore open the Sour Fizz and poured a little pile onto her tongue. She winced and almost coughed as the powder reacted in her mouth.

I laughed watching her do this, but just then a strange wave of light-headedness made my vision swim. There were spots in my eyes, and this weird floaty feeling in my skull, sort of like I didn't even know where I was. I had to put my hand down to steady myself....

Everything got jumbled, and this wave hit me and I felt so sad, and there was a little fluttering panic in my chest, a feeling like I had just lost something really important...tears brimming, heart racing like it might burst—

Then it passed. The world seemed right side up again.

"Here, Penny, try these," I said, holding out the package of Star Chews.

"What?"

I looked up and saw Judy peering at me.

"Oh, sorry, Judy, I, um..." For some reason, I was

holding my hand out to my left, as if there were someone else here with the two of us.

Also, my hand was empty. I flexed my fingers.

Hadn't I been holding something?

"What are you doing?" Judy asked.

"Oh, nothing." I rubbed my head. What had I been doing?

"Do you feel all right?" Judy got to her feet, crouched beside me, and put her hand on my forehead. "You're still kinda warm. I think you're feverish from going through that doorway. Which is why I'm going to forgive you for calling me Penny."

"Sorry, I, um . . ." Penny? I felt like I could picture her right here with us. Like she had been here, the whole time. But that was impossible. "I guess I just wished she were here."

It was times like these—adventures when me and Judy and the Robot found things like this doorway—that made me miss Penny the most.

Except it *also* felt true that she really had just been here. Like I could picture both of those possibilities in my head, and they both seemed like they were real.

Judy stood. "She definitely would have thought this was cool. Although you can almost guarantee she would have used this doorway to do something reckless again."

Like the candy, I thought, looking at the cave floor in front of me. What candy? *The candy we were eating with Penny.* I remembered us laughing and passing it around.

Okay, this was getting weird. Why was I thinking of eating candy here in this cave with Penny; why could I almost picture it when Penny had never been here with us?

But then I realized that I was probably thinking of candy because that was what got Penny in so much trouble back on Earth. Just a few months before we were supposed to leave, she'd gotten caught on surveillance cameras stealing candy from Corner Market, and she'd been expelled from the colony program. *What could you possibly have been thinking?* I remembered Mom saying, tears streaming down her face. *That's not even me!* Penny had shouted back. *Look at what I'm wearing! I don't even own those clothes!* She'd been so adamant, and I'd wanted to believe her, we all had, but in the end it hadn't mattered.

After that, we almost didn't leave Earth at all, but then Mom had been able to get Penny's case reviewed, and after tons of meetings and signed forms, Penny was finally reinstated, except by then it was too late: Her spot on the twenty-fourth mission of the *Resolute* had already been given to someone else. There was room for her on the next mission, but that wouldn't be for two whole years. And so Dad had volunteered to stay and wait with her.

We'd had to say good-bye to the two of them at the spaceport, everyone hugging and crying,

Mom trying to reassure us that it would be okay, that the time would fly by.

Except then the attack on the *Resolute* had happened, and I remembered that moment after the crash when me and Judy and Mom had realized that we might never get back, that we might never see Dad and Penny again. We'd wondered: Had word gotten back to Earth? Did the colonial program have any idea where we'd ended up? We still didn't know. At least if they'd been here with us, we would've all been lost together.

But Dad was here. Penny, too! I thought, and it felt so true. What was happening to me? I figured I was getting things mixed up because I had just time traveled. Anybody's brain would be confused after that. And yet, I could picture both Penny and Dad in my memories, as if they'd actually been here, but then at the same time I could also picture them *not* being here. There we were, on the *Resolute* with them and without them. Crashing on this planet with and without, and on and on. Even this cave…

I looked at Judy, who was taking photos of the doorway with her communicator. "Hey," I said, "does anything seem weird to you?"

"What do you mean?"

"I don't know, like, with your memories? Like about Penny and Dad?"

Judy's eyes narrowed. "What are you talking about?"

"I, um, I swear I can remember Penny being here with us. I know that sounds crazy…."

Judy nodded slowly. Did she remember it, too? But then she said, "I think that doorway really messed with you. I want to get you back and run a more thorough checkup."

"Okay." So it was just me. Which meant Judy was probably right. I'd traveled through space and time. Who knew what that would do to a human brain?

"You feel good enough to head back yet?" Judy asked. "We need to tell Mom about this thing. She could use some good news. We all could."

"Yeah, I guess." I stood up. My head swam again, and I had that strange feeling like nothing made sense.

Judy started up the tunnel. I followed her but stopped and turned back to the doorway. "Coming?" I said to the Robot—

But the Robot wasn't there. Of course he wasn't! As much as I still wished otherwise, Mom had made me send him away two days ago, after the other colonists had convinced her he was too dangerous.

Except I also remembered him being right here with us in this cave. Standing there, saying *Danger*, while Penny and I went through the doorway.

I pictured Penny again, putting on the harness and going through the doorway into some dark place. Where had she gone? The memories were hard to follow, especially because at the same time, I remembered her *not* being here.

"Will," Judy called from up the tunnel. "Come on."

But as I caught up to her, my thoughts kept fighting with each other. *The Robot and I came here. We had to hide from those mothasaurs.* Except I also remembered coming here on my own, and yes, hiding from the creatures, but by myself. *No! We were hiding out in the tunnel entrance*, I thought as I reached the top of the tunnel.

We were right here playing tic-tac-toe!

I stopped and peered at the ground by the cave entrance, sure that I would see a grid drawn in the dirt, but there wasn't one.

CHAPTER

8

We made our way back to camp: across the log bridge, through the forest. As we went, my head started to feel clearer. It had been so weird back there in the cave, the way my thoughts had been so mixed up. But the fresh air and the sunlight helped. Still, I looked over my shoulder. Had I heard something? A mothasaur? Or was I looking for the Robot or Penny, even though, obviously, they weren't with us?

Judy was probably right. Going through that doorway had scrambled my brain. Here in the forest, it was also hard to believe that I'd really been back in my old room, but I rubbed my jacket pocket and the bump of Captain Quasar.

We reached the clapping flowers and I smacked my hands, activating the carpet of magenta blooms. That made me smile, except then I had a weird memory of Penny's face lighting up the first time we'd discovered these. Another impossible thing, but it felt so real.

Also, picturing that made a fresh wave of anger well up inside me. I still couldn't believe Mom had ordered me to send away the Robot! After the rest of the colonists had seen him in the fight with the mothasaurs at the light tower, they'd taken a vote, and even though Mom had tried to talk them out of it, I remembered seeing the worry in her eyes and feeling like she was probably happier with this result anyway. I'd had to walk the Robot to the edge of camp and order him to go away, and he'd stood there for a moment, his face lights still, like he didn't understand, like he didn't want to leave…but he'd followed my command, just like he always did, and I'd been alone ever since.

Except I also remembered Dad fighting for him to stay, convincing the colonists that the Robot was more help than harm. And I remembered the Robot helping me pull circuit boards and explore the trails with me, but those memories seemed foggy, almost distant, and besides they couldn't be true, even if they felt true—

"Will." I turned to see Judy standing close to the water's edge, looking over her shoulder at me. "Where are you going?"

"What do you mean?"

She cocked her head. "Camp is *this* way." She pointed with her thumb down the shore of the lake.

I looked in front of me, up the slope. Judy was right, of course: Our camp was that way, at the *Jupiter 11*. So why was I going this way? *Because that's where our ship is, the* Jupiter 2. Except, of course, it wasn't. The *Jupiter 2, our Jupiter,* was long gone. We'd lost it when the glacier had collapsed. I remembered standing at the edge of the crevasse with Mom and Judy as we watched our ship plummet into the darkness with a massive crash of ice. Why had I been thinking otherwise?

Because I also remembered Dad flying us out of that collapsing ice, flying us to safety, parking the ship at the top of this very hill…but now I realized that there was no trail in front of me, just vegetation, while there was a well-trodden path in the direction that Judy was pointing.

I shook my head and jogged over to her. "Sorry."

"Still feeling weird?"

"Yeah. I've been having these moments where it's like I remember stuff that didn't happen."

Judy frowned. "This is what I was worried about. I shouldn't have let you go."

I followed along behind her, my thoughts still jumbled. Even though I kept seeing proof right in front of me that those other thoughts about Penny and the Robot and Dad weren't real, they still felt like they were. I wondered if maybe because the doorway had scanned my thoughts and feelings, it had scrambled me so that things I'd imagined or wished for now seemed like they'd happened, you know, like those times when you wake up from a dream and you're sure it was real.

That made sense, but it didn't change how real it seemed in my head. Plus, I was still feeling a little dizzy, and the hike back up to our actual camp wasn't helping. As we neared the top of the hill, I glanced over my shoulder—maybe I was confused and looking for the Robot again?—when something moved in the corner of my eye. For just a second, I saw a blurry movement on the trail behind us, and the branches and leaves rustled. I blinked and looked at that spot, but then everything was still. I checked again a few steps later but didn't see anything.

The path led to a clearing where the *Jupiter 11* was parked. This was the ship that Hiroki's family lived in. They'd been nice enough to let us stay with them after we lost our *Jupiter*. I glanced back at the distant mountains and those high glaciers where the *Jupiter 2* was buried, and remembered those terrifying moments of that first night: crashing in water, Judy getting stuck after she went to get the batteries when I panicked, my hike up to the top of the mountain to get magnesium that I thought would help melt the ice. Another double memory flashed in my mind, of Dad and me hiking up there together. I did remember *wishing* he'd been there, being freaked out on that mountain by myself. And then I'd fallen down the crevasse that dumped me out below the glaciers, in the forest where I met the Robot. He'd saved Judy and helped us get into the *Jupiter 2*, but we'd had to abandon it after the glacier became unstable.

Luckily, we'd found Hiroki and his daughter, Naoko, and granddaughter, Aiko. They were so nice and generous, but it was definitely difficult having to share space, food, and supplies.

"There they are!" I heard Mom say.

She and Hiroki were standing outside, huddled around a tablet. Mom was pointing to the afternoon sun, and Hiroki was nodding.

"What's up, guys?" said Judy.

"Nothing," Mom said tightly, in that way she did that always meant the opposite. "We're just doing some tests. How are you guys?"

"We're good," I said immediately.

"Sort of," said Judy. "Will took me to this cave he found, and there's something there that you need to see. Something amazing."

"Amazing, huh?" said Mom, consulting her tablet. "Well, I'd love to come exploring with you guys, but right this moment it will have to wait. I just called Victor. We're going to have a meeting in about twenty minutes with all the survivors. I'd like you guys to be there."

"Sounds serious," said Judy.

"Yes...it is." Mom turned away and it looked like she wiped her eyes.

"The girls left out some food if you want it," Hiroki said.

"Thanks." Judy stood in place for a minute. "Any chance we can get a preview of this big serious thing you want to tell us?"

Mom shook her head. "Inside."

"Come on," I said to Judy, and tugged her arm toward the hatch. We went to the galley, grabbed cheese-pasta protein packs, and took them to the cockpit, where we sat in the big chairs, with the view out over the lake. Mom had scolded us more than once for eating in here, but she seemed too busy to notice.

"Huh," Judy said as she peeled open her pack. "Considering I haven't eaten since breakfast, I'm weirdly not hungry."

"That's because—" I caught myself as I realized it was happening again: My thoughts were sliding around, and I found myself remembering eating candy in the cave with Penny. I even remembered Judy singing, *"Cocoa Pandas in a tree..."*

"What, you think the doorway messed with me, too?" said Judy. "Just from being near it?"

"Maybe," I said. All of a sudden, I felt tears stinging at the corners of my eyes.

Judy heard me sniffle. "Hey, what is it?"

"I just wish Dad and Penny were here," I said.

Judy rubbed my back. "Me too. I know I used to complain about Penny a lot, and I was very used to Dad not being around at all, but..."

I nodded and wiped my nose. "I keep having these memories of them being here, like, with us."

Judy frowned. "I am a bad doctor letting you go

through that doorway. It might also be dehydration, and then of course there are the unknowns of acclimating to this planet's exact atmosphere and gravity. My point is, there are plenty of reasons not to feel normal around here. You should drink some water."

"Okay," I said.

"Kids?" Mom leaned in the doorway, her face serious. "Meeting time."

"Whatever this is," Judy said to me as we stood, "she is super wound up about it."

We trailed after Mom and saw that Hiroki, Naoko, and Aiko were gathered in the common room, along with Victor, his wife, and their son, Vijay. Dr. Smith was there, too, along with Don and a couple of other colonists. Everyone stood around the central table, where Mom had set up a holographic animation that showed what I assumed was this planet orbiting around its star.

"How did it go with the fuel run?" Mom asked.

"Right where I said it would be," said Don, pointing his thumbs at himself. "A *Jupiter* with a full tank of fuel." He winked at Judy, and I saw her roll her eyes.

Mom just nodded.

"I thought that might earn some smiles," said Don, "maybe a robust round of thank-yous."

"As if any number could ever be enough," said Victor, eyeing him.

"It's a big help," Mom said to Don. "Where's the fuel now?"

"Parked safely at our camp," said Victor, crossing his arms. "Now, what was so important that you asked us to risk traveling before dusk, Robinson? Hopefully a spot of good news for once."

Mom bit her lip. "Unfortunately, no." She glanced at Hiroki, who nodded to her. "Hiroki and I have been observing some strange features of this planet's orbit since we arrived. You may have noticed

that the sun tracks oddly in the sky from one day to the next…."

"I think most of us have been too busy with the day-to-day business of survival to look at the sky," said Victor.

"Of course," said Mom, smiling thinly.

"There are odd signs on the surface, too," said Hiroki, pushing up his glasses. "The trees of this planet, despite their size, only have one growth ring, as if they are only a single year old."

"So?" said Victor. "We've already established that this planet's year is much longer than on Earth. What does any of this have to do with us?"

"A lot, it turns out," said Mom. "The data was so odd that I had a look with the high-altitude survey balloon and…" Her face fell as she activated the animation. It showed the planet moving around the sun, and as it got closer in its elliptical orbit, we could see this strange dark circle warping the shape of the star. "There's a black hole off the shoulder of this star. Its position and gravitational effect have warped this planet's orbit such that at its periapsis—"

"I'm sorry, its what?" said Victor.

"Periapsis is the closest point of a planet's orbit to its star," I said.

"That's right, Will." Mom smiled at me, except her eyes were also welling up. "Because of the black hole, when we reach that point, we'll be so close to the star that it will burn all life right off the surface."

"Nothing will survive," said Hiroki.

Victor rubbed his son's shoulder. "You're sure about this?"

"All the models check out," said Mom.

"How long do we have?"

"There's still some question of timing," said Hiroki. "Months, we think. But it could be less. Maybe only weeks."

"Well, that is indeed ominous," said Victor, "but other than scaring us further, it does nothing to change our primary plan to leave this place as quickly as possible and return to the *Resolute*. Perhaps this will put a spring in our collective step."

"True, but it means we don't have another option…" Mom paused, choking up.

"Why do I feel like there's more bad news coming?" asked Don.

Mom nodded and glanced at the ceiling. "We've also been running the numbers, and…" Her eyes flashed to me and Judy, and she turned away, patting Hiroki's shoulder.

"With the number of available *Jupiter* craft that we have," Hiroki continued, "there is not enough room to get everyone off the planet."

"How is that possible?" said Victor. "We could fit dozens of people on any one of these ships if we wanted."

"Space-wise, yes, but each person adds weight,

and the amount of fuel we have on each *Jupiter*, even with the extra stores you just recovered, is barely enough to get each craft off world with minimum crew."

"How short are we?"

A tragic smile crossed Mom's face. "One," she said. "One more *Jupiter* would've been enough to do it. The numbers are so close, but it just won't work."

A pit opened up in my stomach. Our *Jupiter*, lost in the ice—

No, it's not! Memories flooded my mind, of our *Jupiter* safely by the lakeside, of Dad, of Penny—

But it wasn't true. They weren't here, our ship was gone, and without it, there was no escape.

CHAPTER
9

So, if I'm hearing you correctly," said Victor, "you're saying that crashing your ship up in that glacier has doomed us all."

"Hey!" Judy shouted. "It wasn't our fault! The ship was on autopilot and damaged. There was nothing we could have done!"

"So you say," said Victor.

"Yeah, we do!" Judy pointed at him. "You have a lot of nerve—"

"Judy!" Mom snapped. "That's enough. Arguing

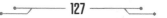

won't help us right now." Her eyes narrowed at Victor. "Neither will placing blame."

As I listened, it felt like my brain was splitting in two. I pictured our *Jupiter* tumbling out of sight into that crevasse, while at the same time I remembered Dad flying it out through the falling ice. Both things seemed real, even though that was impossible!

"Will?"

I blinked and found that I'd stumbled into Judy. My head ached, and there were spots of light in my vision.

"Sorry," I said as she put her arm around me.

"Wait, wait, wait, hold on a second," Don was saying. "We just risked our lives bringing back that whole tank of fuel, and you're saying it doesn't matter?"

"It will help," said Mom, "but even if we spread it among the *Jupiter*s we have, we can't make the numbers work. At least, not yet. Hiroki and I have been running simulations on how to shed weight: what supplies and systems we can dump so that we can accommodate everyone and escape this planet's gravity...."

"That sounds like there's a *but*," said Don.

Mom shrugged. "Even if we find a model that works, it's going to barely work."

"And you're sure there are no other options?" said Victor.

"If we can contact the *Resolute*, they may have a *Jupiter* left that's in working order, and if they can send it down to us, that would do it. If not..."

"If not..." Victor echoed. "What are you implying: that we're going to have to draw straws?"

"That would absolutely be the last option," said Mom.

"But you're saying we might," said Don.

Murmurs rushed around the room, people shaking their heads and rubbing one another's shoulders supportively.

"Obviously, we'll keep doing more tests," said Mom. "As many as it takes."

My chest tightened, like I could barely breathe. "This isn't right," I said.

Judy put her arm around me. "No kidding," she said quietly.

"No," I said, "I mean, really. This can't be right...."

"So that's it, then," said Victor. "And what are we supposed to do in the meantime while you're running numbers?"

"You can do an inventory of each of your ships and weigh everything that can be left behind," said Mom. "We also still need to double-check the thrusters and launch systems. We don't know what damage may have been caused when we evacuated the *Resolute*. That way we're ready if—*when*—we find a solution."

Victor put an arm around Vijay, the other around his wife. "Well, if that's everything, we'll be leaving." He turned them toward the door.

"I could use your help," said Mom. "Running the models."

"I need to get my family to safety before night-fall," said Victor. "We got the fuel. We did our part." They walked out.

"Such a courageous leader," said Don, watching him go.

Mom sighed. "Thanks for coming, everyone. We'll get back to it. And if anyone comes up with another way to contact the *Resolute*, we're all ears."

"We'll tell her about the doorway in the morning," said Judy. "Right now we should see if she needs our help—"

But I stepped away, fighting another wave of dizziness. "I think I need some air."

Judy looked at me with that concerned face again. "Don't go far," she said. "I want to run some more tests on you after I check in with Mom."

I nodded and walked calmly out of the room, but by the time I was at the hatch I was nearly running. I jumped down the steps two at a time and sprinted away from the ship.

The sun had set, and the sky had turned to pale lavender. There were deep shadows beneath the trees and the camp lights had come on. I stopped at the perimeter they made and sat on a large rock, my heavy breaths making clouds. The lake glittered in moonlight, the ice caps on the distant mountains sparkling. This place looked so much like Earth... and yet it wasn't, and now we might die here.

More dizziness washed over me, and I had that sensation of having two memories at once. I had this vision of hiking through the woods with Penny and Judy and the Robot, on our way to the cave, a memory that never was. When would these weird thoughts stop happening? Or had the doorway messed me up permanently?

I rested my elbows on my knees, my chin in my hands as I stared at the ground. Feeling upset wasn't doing me any good. I needed to stop thinking about how I wished things were and deal with how they *really* were. I could help Mom run the numbers, analyze the *Jupiters'* systems, and work the problem.…

In a minute. I didn't feel quite ready yet. I bent down and scooped up a handful of the flat rocks scattered around my feet and hurled one into the dark shadows of the trees, listening as it cracked against an unseen trunk. I threw another, then another.…

But then I paused. A low sound had reached my ears, almost like distant thunder. There was a screech, and a flock of something lifted from the trees by the lake. I turned and scanned the dim horizon, but I didn't see any storm clouds.

Actually, it sounded more like—

"Victor!" Footsteps slammed down the stairs. I spun to see Mom hurtling outside, shouting into her communicator. "What are you doing? Answer me!"

"Heat signatures!" Judy shouted from the hatch, sprinting after Mom.

"What's going on?" I called.

"Fire up the chariot!" said Mom.

"We won't get there in time!"

"Judy, just do it! If we don't stop him…"

She didn't need to finish. Judy sprinted across the camp and wrenched open the chariot door.

"Wait, I'm coming with you!" Don raced out of the *Jupiter*, following Judy.

"Victor!" Mom shouted again. "Please don't do this!"

"Mom, what is it?" I called.

"Victor's powering up his *Jupiter*. He must have loaded the spare fuel. I can't believe him!"

"He's leaving?" I said in disbelief.

"He's trying," said Mom. "Victor! Please listen to me: We haven't run diagnostics on your ship to be sure all the systems are ready for a takeoff."

"I'm sorry, Maureen," Victor finally replied. "We'll send help as soon as we reach the *Resolute*. I've weighed the scenarios you proposed and decided this is the best way; I'm certain of it. Someone needs to get off this planet to get us help. It's my call."

"Oh, come on—"

The chariot peeled out and promptly skidded to a halt beside Mom.

"Will, stay here!" she called, jumping in. "Go!"

The chariot kicked up a cloud of dust and tore off down the trail toward Victor's camp, its lights weaving through the trees.

I sat back down, stunned. The rumbling continued, getting steadily higher in pitch. I felt it in the rock and the ground.

And now a brilliant light ignited in the distance. It grew like a dome, illuminating a tower of smoke, and the circular light pattern of Victor's *Jupiter* rose into the sky. It hovered above the smoke, then eased forward, accelerating. It flew out across the lake, making an arc upward, the angle getting steeper, and steeper still, until it was shooting vertically into the sky, a streak of light against the twilight, burning toward the stars—

BAM! A flash, a fireball. I shielded my eyes.

When I looked up again, I saw glowing embers raining down. From here they looked almost gentle, some snuffing out in the lake, some making blooms of fire in the forest, but I knew what they really were: flaming pieces of spaceship.

Victor. His family...Oh no.

And along with them, the extra fuel and our only chance of escape. This couldn't be happening! I scanned the sky, looking for any sign of a ship still flying higher. Maybe they'd just lost a booster or something....

"Will," Mom said quietly over the communicator.

"Mom," I said, fighting back tears.

"You saw the crash."

"I did, but—was it the whole ship? Or—"

"It was." Mom was silent for a minute. "We—um, we're going to go check the wreckage for survivors. They may have been able to evacuate."

"Okay."

"I don't know how long it will take."

"I know."

I sat there, stunned and crying at the same time.

Quiet seemed to press all around me. I felt so lonely, like I was the last person in the universe. The glow from the crash debris dimmed. The sky was almost dark now. A cold breeze rushed down from the mountains. I wished I was out there with Mom and Judy, but then again I wasn't sure if I wanted to see what they might find. Instead, I pictured my room back home, felt the warmth of our house, us all together, and I wanted more than anything to be there again....

I got out my video recorder and tapped the most recent video from this afternoon, when I'd taken Judy back to the cave.

I am about to officially activate the doorway. It felt like forever ago. I watched as my fingers appeared on the screen and pressed into that liquid-like surface, and then the stars rippled and blurred until I saw my old room again.

No way, Penny said off-camera.

That's impossible, Judy added.

I'm glad you guys can see it, too, I said. *I was wondering if maybe I'd been losing my mind.*

If you are, then we are, too, said Penny—

Wait a minute.

I paused the recording, slid the navigation bar back a few seconds, and played it again.

No way.

That was Penny's voice. But it couldn't be—

If you are, then we are, too. That was definitely her!

And all of a sudden I could picture it, standing there in the cave, making my video with Penny and Judy behind me, and then...

And then...

Penny had gone through the portal! And come back with candy!

But *no, she didn't!* Because if she'd really been there with us, then that meant Dad had been here, too, but there was no trail to our *Jupiter,* and Mom had *just said* that we'd lost that ship, and I knew that Penny and Dad were still on Earth. So how could her voice be in this video?

Unless…

I returned to the recorder menu and scrolled back through my videos to one from yesterday, inside the *Jupiter.* I pressed PLAY. It was a video of me trying to teach the Robot to make a thumbs-up sign.

Like this, I was saying to him—

But wait! The Robot wasn't even here yesterday! And then the camera moved and Penny walked by. She gave a side-eye to my thumbs-up and to the Robot. *Dork,* she said.

I stopped the video. Scrolled to another, fingers shaking. How was this possible? She'd been here. The Robot had been here. And then:

Will. There was Dad, in a video from two days ago. He was bent and peering into a compartment in the *Jupiter. Stop recording and get me a thermal wrench,* he said.

Dad, too! And that wasn't Hiroki's *Jupiter*. It was *ours*!

I had to stop and ask myself: Was I going insane? Was I really seeing this, or had my brain gotten even more scrambled by the doorway than I thought? How could this be real—

But then I realized I'd had the camera with me, in my pocket, when I'd gone through the doorway. I came back with weird memories, and *it* came back with these videos. And that could only mean one thing: All these things had really happened. I hadn't been imagining them or making them up.

But that still left a big question: happened *when*?

And then I remembered that there was a third thing that had gone through the portal: Penny.

I closed my eyes and focused and found that memory: pictured Penny coming back through the portal, dumping an armful of candy on the floor that she stole. If she was there in my head and on the videos, it could only mean one thing.

"We changed the future," I said out loud. Changed it by altering the past. Or…Penny did. When she went through the portal and took the candy, the version of her back on Earth got blamed for it, leading to the situation we were in now!

The realization hit me like an asteroid. Oh man, Judy had been right about the dangers! But she didn't seem to remember this at all. That must have been because unlike me and my camera, she had never actually gone through the doorway. For her, that other past that I remembered had basically never happened.

But if this was really true, how could we change it back? I had to think.…To keep the Penny back on Earth from getting in trouble, I would need to stop the Penny from *here* from stealing the candy. How was I going to do that? Actually, it was obvious: I would have to go back to the same day that Penny had gone to and intercept her. Undo the shoplifting, and everything should go back to the way it used to be.

"Okay," I said, getting to my feet, "we can do this." I smiled. Part of it was relief: I wasn't crazy! But it was also because I could fix this! I wanted to go back to the cave right now—

There was a snapping sound out in the darkness, almost as if the forest had heard my thoughts and wanted to remind me that going now would be a bad idea. There were mothasaurs and who-knew-what-else that we hadn't run into yet, and I didn't even have the Robot.

If you're out there, I thought, *I need you.* I didn't know if the Robot could hear me, wherever he was, or if he'd even want to help me after Mom had made me send him away. It sure would be nice to have him along when we went to the cave, though.

But either way, once I showed Mom and Judy these videos, they would definitely want to come with me. Maybe even Hiroki, too. Especially after what had happened to Victor and his family— they'd definitely agree that this was a risk worth taking. And it would be wise for me to wait for them, not just because daytime was safer, but also so we could really think this through.

"We're going to be okay." Saying those words made me feel the best I had all day, so good I had to shout it. "We're going to be okay!" My voice echoed across the lake.

Another snap in the bushes, louder this time. Closer.

"Okay, fine, I get it," I said, still smiling. It was time to head back inside and wait for Mom and Judy to get back.

I turned toward the ship—

And froze. I peered at the ground, and then flashed the light from my communicator.

There was a footprint in the dirt. It was large and round, and I wanted to doubt it, but I knew immediately where I had seen ones just like it before.

Then I heard a sizzling sound behind me. I turned and saw something at the edge of the clearing, like a ripple in my vision that made the trees behind it look blurry. It was like I had something in my eye, but I blinked and nothing changed, so I flicked one of the rocks I was still holding in that direction—

The spot shimmered, and white sparks showered to the ground. There was a flash of bright light in the shape of a large, humanlike figure dressed in a long black cloak, a hood over its head, and wearing thick goggles with round eyepieces that reflected in the sparks. The figure disappeared almost as quickly as it had appeared, but not before I could tell that it was coming right toward me.

Run! I spun and started toward the *Jupiter* hatch, but almost immediately skidded to a halt. There were more footprints between me and the steps. I flung the last rock I had toward the entrance—

Another shower of sparks, and a second figure in a heavy cloak flashed into sight right in front of the hatch, waiting to grab me.

CHAPTER

10

elp!" I shouted, and sprinted toward the trees. I careened down the trail, stumbling over the rocky ground. As I ran, I stabbed at my communicator, turning on my flashlight.

I reached the tree line and glanced over my shoulder, but I couldn't see anything. I bent and grabbed a rock. Spun, threw it straight behind me—

Zap! One of the figures was right there, reaching for me.

I turned and ran as hard as I could, the light bobbing in front of me, my legs wheeling. Down the zigzagging trail to the lakeside. I grabbed another rock and twisted and threw it, but my throw went wide. *Just like when Coach tried to play me at shortstop.* I just knew they were still there and I kept on sprinting, my feet pounding as branches whipped against my arms and legs.

Thoughts blurred through my mind, too fast to answer: Who were they? *Probably aliens.* Why were they after me? *Because I'd used the doorway.* What did they want? *To capture me or kill me or both!*

I reached the grove of clapping flowers, all curled up tight in the dark. Ahead was the trail that led to the caves, but that was probably the last place I wanted to go. Maybe if I went up the hill—

Suddenly, light flashed all around me, and I felt a surge of electricity, like I'd been shocked. I tripped and crashed to the ground.

I rolled over onto my side, blinking at the brightness, trying to get my feet back under me, but something heavy pushed me down. I waved my communicator light and saw the forest blur. Clawing at the nearby ground, I found a branch and threw it straight up. It flashed in a burst of sparks. One of those figures was right there, looming over me. It was so close now that I could see that its goggles were glowing with a deep red light from inside.

"Leave me alone!" I shouted.

A heavy grip yanked me up by my shoulder, and as soon as the figure touched me, it appeared in full view.

"Let me go!" I struggled, but I couldn't break free— WHUMP!

The figure's grip released and it flew backward, becoming invisible again. Ferns and flowers were crushed where it hit the ground.

I stumbled back and slammed into something solid, metal, and warm.

My Robot!

"Hey!" I shouted. "You came!"

He looked at me with his blue starlit face. I hadn't

seen him in days, but then in my other memories it had only been hours. Which one was it for him?

He pushed me firmly behind him and then swung his fist again, as if at nothing, but there was a shower of sparks and the second one of those figures went flying.

Then the Robot whirled around, lifted me onto his back, and took off up the hill with long, bounding strides.

"I'm so glad you found me," I said to him. I looked behind us but couldn't tell if any of those figures were back there. Another wave of dizziness washed over me, and I leaned against the Robot and stared out at the dark woods.

He ran until we reached the top of the hill, and he stopped in a clearing and bent to let me down.

"Are we safe?" I said, peering into the trees behind us. The Robot's head panned back and forth, scanning.

I sat down hard on the dirt. Moonlight reflected

on the water below. I saw the lights of the camp at Hiroki's *Jupiter* across the lake. Far off in the distance, a few fires were still burning from Victor's crash. I saw lights sweeping around out there, too: Mom and Judy and Don, maybe other colonists, searching for survivors.

"Where have you been?" I asked, my voice barely more than a croak. "Something pretty crazy has happened."

He still didn't look at me.

"I'm sorry I sent you away, but it wasn't really me—well, I mean, it was me, but I didn't want to, and there's another reality where I don't."

The Robot's head paused from his scanning. "Danger," he said.

"Do you remember that? The other timeline I'm talking about?"

The Robot surveyed the forest one more time and then clomped over. With a hum of servos, he knelt beside me. His face lights were making the figure-eight pattern, and now a small light began to flicker on the side of his head. The light formed into a picture on the ground in front of us, a three-dimensional image like a hologram. I saw a figure sitting on the ground in the dark and realized it was me. There was someone else sitting there: Judy. We were looking at something, and I realized that it was the doorway in the cave.

"This is from..." My thoughts clicked into place. "You remember it, too! You remember being there!" And now I could picture him there, with that strange flickering light, his own version of my video recorder.

In the recording, Judy and I were talking.

Does she have any idea the kind of trouble she could cause? I heard Judy ask. *Is she even thinking of how worried we are?*

She probably doesn't realize how long she's been gone, I said.

"This was the first time," I said to the Robot. "This is when it happened."

The Judy in the hologram pointed at the doorway. *There she is!*

And then the doorway flashed, and Penny stumbled back into the cave. Even though I remembered this, it was a huge relief to see it happening outside of my own memories.

What were you thinking? Judy said, and then Penny replied, *Having a genius moment,* and she opened her arms and dumped a mess of candy onto the cave floor. *Behold!*

"You recorded this because you *knew*, didn't you?" I said to the Robot. "But how did you save it? You didn't actually go through the portal...then again, you are a super-advanced alien being who can probably detect changes in space-time like this."

"Danger."

"Yeah, you were right. Believe me, I see that now."

Did you steal this? Judy was saying in the Robot's recording.

Well, I mean, sort of? But it wasn't even really me, right? I was still in school, so . . .

But it was you, Penny! Judy was shouting. *If you'd been seen, if you'd gotten caught—*

"She did get caught," I said to the Robot. "You know that, too, don't you?"

A moment later, there was a weird glitch in the video feed, like a bolt of static ripping across the picture, and when it cleared, Penny and the candy were gone.

Here, Penny, try these, the me in the recording said, holding out his hand, but his hand was empty.

And then the footage abruptly ended. The little light on the Robot's head stopped flickering.

"That was the moment, wasn't it?" I said. "When Penny's shoplifting changed the past. I remember the other her, the one in the past on Earth, denying it, but of course no one believed her. And there was no way anyone ever could have imagined the truth. And Penny was so depressed after, she kept insisting she hadn't done it...." I remembered her sulking around the house in those months before we left. She'd even gotten kicked out of the school play because the stealing had happened during that dress rehearsal.

"And now everything's gotten worse with the colonists," I said. "Did you see Victor's *Jupiter* crash?" I pointed toward the distant wreckage, and the Robot looked in that direction. "You and me are the only ones who know about this. We have to change it back."

The Robot's face lights started flowing toward the center.

Something cracked in the trees nearby. The Robot turned toward it. "Danger," he said.

"Those aliens showed up right after I thought about using the doorway to go back and stop Penny." I remembered something Judy had said when we first found the doorway, about how it had to be scanning our brains. "Maybe now they can hear my thoughts," I said. "Maybe they've been watching us since we left the cave, and when I thought about using the doorway again, they wanted to stop me. You can see them, can't you?"

The Robot kept scanning the edge of the clearing.

"Can you get me back to Hiroki's ship? It's probably a little safer there."

The Robot turned and held out his hands. I stood, and this time he lifted me up and put me on his shoulders. He started to jog back down the hill toward the trail.

I kept my eyes peeled for blurring but didn't see any. Maybe the aliens didn't want to mess with the Robot again. Or maybe they were busy coming up with a way to stop him, and it would only be a matter of time before they returned.

CHAPTER

11

The Robot stepped to the edge of the camp and paused, just within the shadows of the trees. The chariot was still gone, which meant Mom and Judy weren't back yet.

"What is it?" I said.

The Robot motioned toward the hatch of the *Jupiter*. I squinted, and a second later I saw the slightest blur. "They're still here," I whispered.

The Robot retreated slowly into the shadows.

"Will!" Hiroki was waving to us from down in the trees, behind a pile of boulders. We moved

quietly over and saw that his daughter and granddaughter were with him.

"Your family was asking about you," Hiroki
said as we arrived. "They will be glad to know that
you're all right." Hiroki gave me that gentle smile
that he always managed to have, one that helped
calm me down in almost any situation.

"Have they found any survivors?" I asked.

"So far, no luck. I have not told them yet about
this." Hiroki pointed to the blur by the hatch.
"They came on board, looking around. Aiko was
the first to spot them." He rubbed his granddaughter's shoulder. Her eyes flashed at me, but she
looked quickly away, and I noticed that she was
shaking.

"They didn't seem interested in us," Hiroki
added, "but we thought it best not to stick around.
I take it you know what those things are?"

"Yeah," I said. I tapped the Robot and he let me
down, and we crouched beside Hiroki. "They're

from a cave that me and Judy"—I almost said *and Penny* but I stopped myself—"found. Well, from a doorway inside that cave."

"A doorway?" said Hiroki.

"It kinda lets you move through time. And space."

"I see...." Hiroki nodded toward the blurry being. "Their presence also suggests that you have used this doorway."

"Kinda?" I said.

"And are you now going to tell me that this current moment has been altered from what it might have been?"

"How did you know?"

Hiroki smiled. "I didn't. But it was the natural supposition from what you've already said. If such a doorway really does exist, it seems almost impossible that you would not at least test it. It's what almost any human would have done."

"Judy didn't. My mom probably wouldn't."

"Don't be so sure. Especially given our current predicament."

"What we did changed things," I began, and I told him what I knew about Penny's trip through the door, and what had happened.

Hiroki took off his glasses and cleaned them on his sleeve. "It's strange....I have been experiencing more than a usual amount of the feeling that I've been here before. I've often thought that was the sensation, however briefly, of another life lived. Based on what you're saying, I may have been right."

"I don't know if things are a little different or a lot different," I said, "but I do know that we're in more danger than we used to be."

"It is hard to say how many different variables would be changed," said Hiroki. "Every action and condition influences countless others, spreading out across a system. A phenomenon often referred to as the butterfly effect."

"Oh yeah, I've heard of that," I said.

"It is a helpful metaphor," said Hiroki. "No one knows quite how this would play out in terms of altering variables in time, because no one has successfully traveled through time…until you, it seems."

"Yeah, well, I was going to try to change things back. I figured if I went and stopped Penny from stealing the candy, everything would return to the way it was."

Hiroki nodded. "That could work, but it is still dangerous. You would need to be very careful to interact with as little of the world as possible. We have no idea what slight alteration could lead to big changes."

"Sure, no pressure," I said.

"Grandfather," Aiko said quietly, looking at us with wide eyes, "why not go back and warn everyone about the attack on the *Resolute*? Then we might be able to avoid all this in the first place."

"Do you think that would work?" I said.

Hiroki sighed, and a smile crossed his face. "One of the great blessings of the human mind is the ability to wonder, to think *what if*. There would be no problem-solving without it. And yet, it can be a curse as well, when we turn to wondering about our past and how things could have gone differently. The past is to be learned from, but the future is what we should seek to change." Hiroki's brow wrinkled like he was deep in thought.

He drew a dot in the dirt with his index finger and then started drawing concentric circles around it. "Imagine that you change one thing about the past. It is like dropping a stone in a pond, causing waves and ripples of effect through time. When you try to change another thing, you drop a second stone in, and not only are you adding more ripples, those ripples are interacting with the other ripples, and the patterns become increasingly complex. Things could change far beyond what you intend, and there could be many unforeseen consequences. I think, for the moment, we should focus on trying to catch that first stone before it even hits the water. Then we can think about whether or not it is worth trying to make larger changes. That is"—he turned back to the *Jupiter* hatch—"if our new friends will even let you near the doorway again."

"Yeah, I don't think they're going to like that," I said.

Just then, my communicator buzzed. "Will, this is Judy."

"Hey," I said, ducking down behind the bushes.

"Why are you whispering?"

"Just, um…" If I told her about the aliens, that might make her and Mom hurry back here, which would only put more people in danger. "It's late and people are asleep." I could feel Hiroki eyeing me, but he didn't say anything. "How are you guys doing?"

"It's not good," said Judy. "No sign of survivors,

but we'll keep looking. I don't think we'll be back for a few hours, so you should probably try to get some rest."

I glanced up at the ship, at the blurry forms by the stairs. "Yeah, okay."

"Is there something wrong? I mean, besides, you know, everything?"

"Not really."

"At dawn we should tell Mom about the doorway and then take her there. The more I think about it, the more I think using it is the only way to save everyone, though I have no idea how yet."

"Yeah, um...sounds good. See you later. Be careful."

"Thanks. You too."

As I lowered my communicator, the Robot tapped my shoulder and motioned toward the path.

"What?" I said. He motioned again. "You want to go back the way we came—or do you want to go back to the cave?"

His light flowed faster toward the center, and he turned like he wanted me to get on his back.

"But Judy and my mom…" But in this reality, Mom had made me send the Robot away, so on top of everything about the doorway and Penny, I was also going to have to explain what he was doing here.

"I think we're going to go to the doorway now," I said to Hiroki. "The Robot can fight off these guys, and the sooner we fix this, the better."

Hiroki nodded. "I am hesitant to advise you to do something so dangerous, but in this case… good luck. We will keep watch here."

"Thanks. Hopefully when I see you, um…"

He smiled. "We won't even remember that we spoke."

"Right."

CHAPTER

12

I held on to the Robot's shoulders as he loped down the hillside into the dark forest, away from camp. But we hadn't gone ten meters when I started to worry: How were we going to avoid these aliens?

"We should probably stay off the trail," I said, and the words were barely out of my mouth when the Robot turned sharply and started to push through the woods, away from the lakeside and toward the mountains, taking a route that I'd never been on, one that didn't even seem to have a path.

Soon we reached a different section of the

crevasse, but instead of finding a log to lay across it, the Robot leaped over it in one huge stride.

As we went, I tried to formulate a plan: *If* we could get back to the doorway, I was going to need to find Penny on the right day. But which day was that in my memories? The answer might be in my video journal. I was pretty sure I'd made an entry the night that she'd been caught and expelled... except, wait, *this* video recorder showed the other reality, where she didn't get expelled. I closed my eyes and tried to sort the memories....Okay, in that reality, Penny had asked me to get footage of her play on opening night, and I was pretty sure she'd said her dress rehearsal was that morning.

I got out my video recorder and scrolled backward through the files. I had so many, not one from every day, but then sometimes a few on a single day. And it was so strange because I remembered all these moments and yet these were videos of another *reality*, and seeing them gave me that slippery, foggy feeling in my head again. In a way, these moments on my recorder no longer existed, or did they? It made me wonder: If I was able to stop Penny, would this reality cease to exist? And what would happen to this version of me? Did that mean there were two Will Robinsons? The thoughts caused a pit in my stomach. If there could be more than one reality, then which one was actually real?

I took a deep breath. Had to focus! Obviously this was real because here I was, and the danger was real, and there was something real I could do to make things better. I kept scrolling, and the thumbnails of my videos started to play as I passed each one. It was like watching it all in reverse: our time on the *Resolute*, the orbiting space docks above Earth, the rocket ride up there going backward instead, down through the atmosphere, Earth growing bigger as we got closer to the surface, saying hello to our house instead of good-bye, unpacking everything and placing it back in all the rooms. Then there was stuff about school and home and finally I saw a thumbnail of a darkly lit stage. I let it play for a second and there was Penny, reciting Shakespeare, her voice echoing in the auditorium.

The next video was from that morning. Hopefully it was the one I needed to find the memories for intercepting Penny.

I tapped it: *Hey, guys, it's Will. Just checking in to introduce you to my Trash Bot that I made for today's science fair.* The old me held up a little palm-size drone with four propellers and a claw beneath it that was almost as big as its body. That's right! This was from my last science fair (and yes, if you're curious, I won). *It's armed with sensors that will scan the ground for paper and plastic and other materials and then pick them up and bring them to trash cans or recycling bins. You might wonder how it can tell if, say, an item it picks up is actually trash. Well, I made this visual and materials index that the drone can reference.*

Watching this made it all flood back to me: all the hours I'd spent working on that project, winning and how proud Mom had been, and how we'd celebrated that and Penny's show later that night with cake. But then I could also remember coming home with that blue ribbon only to find the house in total despair with Penny's bad news. "Well," I said to the Robot, "at least I win the science fair, no matter what."

I closed my eyes and tried to picture every detail of that morning to make it fresh in my mind. What had I done after that video? Had breakfast, walked to school, went inside early to practice flying the Trash Bot and finish my exhibit poster. The best time to have a time portal show up was probably when I was walking to school. There weren't usually many people around.

Penny and I technically went to different schools, but the middle school and the high school buildings were on the same campus—so I would have a shot at intercepting her.

Of course then I had a dizzying thought: Did that still happen? How could Penny arrive back in time from a future she was never a part of? But she *had* to, didn't she? Or she'd never be there to steal the candy in the first place....I would have to assume that she did because otherwise, I had no idea what to do.

I put my recorder away and noticed that the Robot had slowed down. A few strides later, we arrived at the walls of the cliffside. I was pretty sure we were south of where the doorway was.

"Now what?" I said.

The Robot gripped the rocks and we began to climb, spidering up the cliff, from one outcropping to the next, rising above the treetops. As we went, I noticed scrapes in the rock around the handholds that he was using.

"You've come this way before, haven't you? Is this what you were doing after Mom made me send you away? Mapping out a route to get to the doorway undetected? Nice work."

We climbed until we reached a narrow ledge high above the trees. The Robot started to carefully sidestep along it, over gaps here and there that dropped into darkness. Soon we reached a point where the ledge ended, and the Robot climbed again, and we emerged on a wide plateau in the moonlight. Ahead, I could see a sheer cliff dropping away. I had no idea how we were going to cross that—

But the Robot stopped before we reached it and looked down at his feet. I saw that we were standing over a ragged, triangular hole in the rock.

"Um, do we have to?"

The Robot crouched and started down. After a moment, we were in total darkness. The space narrowed around us, until the rocks were scraping my back and shoulders. We kept descending, and then the Robot let go of the rock and jumped backward slightly. For a second we fell, and I almost screamed, but we landed on what seemed like soft ground. I

aimed my flashlight and saw that there was a narrow, jagged tunnel leading off in either direction,
too tight for the Robot to carry me through, and he
bent so that I could get off him.

I followed him through the darkness, our feet
squishing on the damp ground. The tunnel wound
along, sometimes getting so short that the Robot had
to crawl, sometimes so narrow that we had to walk
sideways. It was pitch-black except for the lights
from his face and my flashlight, and silent except
for the distant rushing of an underground river.

We reached a spot where there were piles of
rock on the floor, and I saw a fissure with fresh,
deep scrapes on either side. The Robot squeezed
into the narrow space that he'd carved.

We slid along through the fissure, the rock tight
on all sides, until it ended at what looked like a solid
wall. The Robot looked up and I saw that there was
a flat crack above our heads, just wide enough to
crawl through. The Robot turned and tapped my

wrist, telling me to turn off my flashlight. Then he cupped his hands like he was making me a step.

"You sure about this?" I said as I put my foot in his hands. He lifted me to the crack. "This is pretty tight." I felt my pulse speeding up as I crawled in.

Rock pressed on my back and my knees. I shuffled forward and couldn't see a thing. The only way that I could tell I was going the right way was a cool breeze against my face. The rock was damp beneath my hands. It scraped my spine and I started to imagine being stuck in here, unable to move, unable to call for help....Suddenly, it felt hard to breathe. I stopped but had this urge, this need, to stand up, to stretch out, except that was impossible. The walls felt like they were too close, getting closer—

I felt a gentle push on my foot and twisted to see the Robot, lying flat so he could fit through.

"Right, sorry," I said, and I took a deep breath and started to crawl forward again.

A few more shuffles and I finally saw light: that

eerie green. The rock around me opened up, and I emerged in the rear of the cave. The doorway was up the slope from me, and beyond that, the tunnel entrance. It was too dim to tell if the aliens were there, but if they were, they'd probably be up by the tunnel, thinking we'd try to get in that way.

I slipped out of the crack and crouched beside it as the Robot emerged, too.

"Do you think the doorway works from both sides?" I whispered. It looked the same from back here, showing a field of darkness and stars.

The Robot looked from me to the doorway.

"Yeah, I think so, too." I started to creep up toward the doorway on my hands and the balls of my feet. I moved diagonally until the doorway and its star view was between me and the tunnel entrance. I stood and stepped toward it, trying not to make a sound.

I had to hope that what we'd theorized about the door would really work. As I got closer, I focused on that one morning, on my walk to school with my Trash Bot, trying to remember every detail I could. I reached out and touched the starry surface with my finger....

The doorway began to ripple, and then space started to blur and zoom past. Into the Milky Way, to our solar system and to Earth, and the view halted on a sidewalk, on a street in the hazy morning sunshine. One of the streets I took on the way to school.

"Okay," I said to the Robot. "Be right back—"

Suddenly, there was a flash of light beside me.

An alien appeared and reached for me. The Robot lunged out of the dark and grabbed its arm and hurled it away, but another one appeared, and another, both grabbing the Robot by the shoulders.

The Robot thrashed and swatted at them with one hand, and with the other he reached for me and shoved me toward the doorway.

I tumbled through the barrier, felt that freezing sensation all over, and then I was through, my feet pounding on the concrete as I caught my balance, sunlight in my eyes.

I stood up and tried to look normal while also seeing if anyone noticed me. But I'd gotten lucky; the sidewalks were empty on both sides of the street.

I spun around and for just a second I saw through the doorway. Three of those aliens were grabbing the Robot from all sides, their red-goggle eyes glowing. He struggled to fight them off, but they were too strong. He yanked one hand free and reached toward the portal with an outstretched finger....

The doorway disappeared. Gone, just like that.

CHAPTER

13

I stood there gaping at the sidewalk where the doorway had been. Had the Robot been able to fight off those aliens, or was he captured now, and if so, what would they do to him? And how was I going to get back? Was I trapped here on Earth, in the past?

Except wait—no. That last part I could handle. I could go back through the doorway when Penny from the cave showed up. At least for the moment, my plans were the same.

I looked around, and all at once, it hit me: the

hot breeze, the heat off the sidewalk, the singed electric odor of traffic buzzing by, and that slightly sour aroma of the haze. Houses, cars, the rustle of synthetic trees in the little yards... Earth. It was almost too much to take.

I heard laughter and saw three kids approaching on the other side of the street. And then a movement caught my eye on this side. A figure had rounded the corner and was walking in my direction. It was my past self, on the way to school.

I ducked and lunged into the space between the bushes along a high fence. Crouching there, I thought, *This is insane!* My past self was about to walk by his future self! Can you imagine if you were just walking along minding your own business and suddenly you saw *you* hiding in the bushes? Of course, I didn't remember seeing myself in the past, but that didn't mean I was safe; Penny had changed the future, so obviously I could, too, if I wasn't careful.

Luckily, as the past version of me got closer, I

saw that he was totally preoccupied with the Trash Bot. He fiddled with it and then it rose into the air in front of him, its little propellers buzzing.

"See what you find!" my past self said. Trash Bot buzzed ahead up the street, right past me. The old me jogged after it, smiling. I clenched, afraid to breathe, but he raced right by me, too.

Then I heard laughter. Across the street, I saw those other kids pointing at my old self and whispering to one another. Misha, Alena, and Stefan—who used to be my friends. Except sometime during sixth grade they'd gotten cool and I hadn't. I remembered that feeling: like someone had taught them a secret language and then they only wanted to hang out together and acted like school was stupid. Which made me feel stupid for thinking that something like a science project was cool. I balled up my fists; even on this morning when I hadn't been thinking about them at all, they'd been making fun of me.

But, sure, even I had to admit running up the street talking to a little robot drone wasn't super high on the cool scale.

I haven't changed that much, I realized, thinking of how I was always talking to the Robot. But then, what did those kids know? They could never befriend an alien robot....

Stop thinking about that! I had to focus. I peered out of the bushes and watched until my past self had crossed the street and entered the school grounds. I had just started to get up when another pair of students appeared on my side of the street. I ducked and waited as they walked by, engrossed in holochats beaming up from their communicators. Once the coast was clear again, I slipped out and headed toward campus. I stayed close to the bushes, hopefully out of sight. Penny's school was on the next block past mine. I'd have to wait until the morning bell rang before I could risk walking by the grounds.

As I got close, I could hear the morning chatter. I stopped at the edge of the fence and peered across the street. There, inside the schoolyard, were groups and clusters of kids, the younger ones running this way and that, climbing all over the playground equipment, the older ones standing in groups talking or shooting basketballs or riding hover boards. I didn't see myself, but then I remembered that my past self was already inside doing last-minute flight tests and finishing my project poster.

A lump started to form in my throat. A tingling sensation in my hands and feet. I hadn't loved school, but looking at all those kids, how happy they seemed, I realized how safe it had been compared to my life now. I remembered climbing on the ropes and bars of the playground structure when I was younger, remembered this very morning, being in the classroom firing up my drone while Ms. Thomas sat behind her desk working.

My only worry in the world had been about a science fair ribbon. Thinking about it all made my eyes start to tear up again.

The bell rang, that same old harsh electric tone that I remembered, and everyone hoisted their packs and started to head inside. Some kids ran for one more turn on the slide. One girl dribbled out and took a final long shot, but soon the yard was nearly deserted except for one group of middle-school boys who were huddled tight and speaking in urgent whispers, probably about lunch credits or gaming coin.

I should go, I thought, but I kept standing there. My whole body felt like it was wound up tight. I had this urge to run across the street and get to class on time, even though it wasn't my class anymore.

A second bell sounded.

"All right, gentlemen!" A teacher appeared, striding toward the last group of boys. Ms. Janila, the music teacher. She glanced at her wrist. "Looks like you'll be heading to the office for late passes."

"Aw, come on!" one of the kids said.

"What can I say? I don't control time." She motioned toward the doors, and the group started inside with their heads hung. Ms. Janila turned to follow them.

I stepped out from the corner and crossed the street. Once I had made it past the yard, I would loop around to the high school auditorium and then find another place to hide until Penny appeared. I had no idea when she'd make her break for it. She'd said *morning,* but that could be in twenty minutes or three hours—

"Will!" I froze. Oh no. Ms. Janila had turned back around and was waving in my direction. "Hey, Mr. Robinson! Let's go! You're late!"

CHAPTER

14

Run! I thought—but if I did that, Ms. Janila would think it was the me from the past ditching school. And then my past self would get in trouble, and who knew how that might change things.

"Come on!" Ms. Janila waved again.

No no no! I raised my hand. "Hey," I said, starting toward her.

I crossed the street and walked through the gate, the whole time feeling like I might explode. When I reached her, she motioned to her communicator.

"I'm sure you're aware that you're late. You'll have to check in at the office."

"Okay," I said, staying where I was and trying not to shake. "Thanks."

"Come on," she said, "I'm headed that way, too."

"Oh, um, right." I fell in step beside her.

"No backpack today?"

"Huh? Oh, no, I mean, it's inside. I just ran back home to get something."

"Ah." She looked at my empty hands, her brow wrinkling. "Didn't find it?"

You're not holding anything! "It was my slideshow for the science presentation. I just had to upload it." The lies were adding up, and it felt like the slightest breeze was going to send them all crashing down.

"That's right—the science fair is today. Nervous?"

"A little bit, I guess."

"I'm sure you'll do great."

We entered the building. There was nobody in the hall, and my classroom was upstairs, but my eyes still darted in every direction. If the wrong person saw me…

"Cool costume, by the way." She motioned to my clothes. "Isn't that a colonial program uniform?"

"Oh, uh, yeah." My insides were twisting in a knot.

"Part of your presentation, too?"

"Yeah, exactly. I, um, I thought it might be cool if…"

"Oh wait, that's right! Your family was selected for a mission!" Now she smiled. "Well, I'd be wearing one, too, if I were you. You guys are lucky." As if on cue, she coughed hard into her arm. "I've had an application in for two years. They say the air quality on Centauri is way better than here. Maybe if I'm lucky, I'll get to be your music teacher there, too."

"That would be cool," I said.

We reached the office and Ms. Janila stepped behind me. I walked in, shaky hands in my pockets.

"Well, I assume you can take it from here," she

said, moving past me and crossing the room. "Have a good day, Will, and good luck with the presentation."

"Thanks." I managed to smile at her. *Finally.* She turned and walked out the door at the far end of the office. Okay, this was my chance. I started to turn—

"Sign in at any terminal." The office manager had noticed me and pointed toward three screens on the counter. This was where you had to officially log in as tardy. Okay...except then I remembered that wasn't going to work, because my earlier self would already have scanned his communicator when he walked into the classroom. "I already signed in," I said. "I, um, just ran home to get something."

"That's fine, just do it again. You're still tardy." She smiled at me for a second before her face fell as she returned to her work.

I moved to a terminal. How was the past version of me going to explain a tardy to my parents? Or worse, was this going to alert my classroom teacher right now? If that happened, things were going to get real confusing, real fast.

"Is there a problem?" The office manager had looked up again, and there was no smile this time.

"Oh, um, no." *Come on, think!*

Then I remembered how when I'd visited my old room, my communicator had flashed that message: INCOMPATIBLE NETWORK. This communicator that I had from the *Resolute* was a different, more advanced model than the ones we'd used at school; I was pretty sure I'd even heard that the entire network system was different. That might mean that if I just did what the office manager said...

I activated my communicator and held it out to the scanner on the screen, holding my breath. A red flash lit up the screen with a loud beep and an error message: ERROR CODE -43: UNKNOWN SOURCE.

"I, uh, think something's wrong with my communicator," I said. "It's been acting up."

The manager huffed and tapped her screen, squinting to read the message. "Try it again."

I did and got the same flashing result.

"Hold on…" She tapped through different screens, probably resetting stuff.

"Okay, now."

I scanned and the error message came up a third time. "Is there a way that I can manually sign in or something?" I said, even adding a smile. You know that trick where you pretend you want to be helpful when you really want the opposite?

"Wait. Hold on…" She tapped some more screens.

Just then the office phone rang.

The manager glanced at her screen and huffed.

"I could come back later," I said, "but I really don't want to miss the science fair."

She tapped the screen again, and whatever came up made her scowl. She waved her hand at me. "Just go. We'll deal with it later." She pressed her earpiece. "Hello, main office?"

I stepped back toward the door, still watching her to be sure....

"Yes," the manager said. "I've been calling you for almost a week. The lunch shipment numbers have been way off, and the online system doesn't seem to be accepting my requests for—uh-huh, no, I know that—"

I turned and hurried out of the office. There was an exit just a little ways down the hall, and I walked quickly toward it. A teacher appeared up ahead and glanced at me—but it was one of the younger-grade teachers I didn't know. I slowed and tried to look calm as we passed by each other, then I veered toward the doors and pushed through.

Outside, down the steps—not spotted yet—to the sidewalk...made it! I rounded the corner and leaned against the wall, catching my breath and feeling like I might faint. That was too close! But had it worked? I closed my eyes and tried to remember: Did I have any memory of getting called for a very confusing tardy on the science project day? Nope. Okay, but-terfly effect avoided! At least for now.

Back to intercepting Penny: The fastest way to the high school auditorium was to go around in front of the schools, but that would take me right past both main entrances. Given how my luck had gone so far, I figured I'd better play it a little safer. If I went a block away from campus, I could loop around on the side streets to the other side of the high school. It would take three times as long, though, so I'd have to move fast.

I walked to the corner, then took off up the street at the fastest walk I could manage without outright running. I felt like I needed to look in all directions at once, in case someone recognized me, but there weren't that many people around at this time of day. Kids were at school and their parents at work. So I forced myself to just look straight ahead, and told myself over and over that no one was going to recognize me.

Besides, with the haze, there were very few people out walking, and anyone driving by had their windows up. I was starting to feel that tickle in my throat that came from breathing this stuff, and I would probably start coughing soon, the way I had so often when I lived here, so much so that I'd needed to use an inhaler.

I rounded the blocks and reached the back side of the high school, within sight of a set of doors that I was pretty sure led to the rear of the auditorium. I stopped on the far corner watching them. After twenty minutes, I was sweating like crazy in my colonial outfit. I was also starting to worry: How long was I going to have to wait, and what if someone from my school came along? Teachers sometimes went to the coffee shop a few blocks away. If someone drove by, I might end up in the office again, only this time they might call Mom.

Thirty minutes later, and the doors still hadn't opened. Meanwhile, it was weird to think that my past self was in the gym at my school presenting the Trash Bot. It had worked so well. I wondered for a second if there was any way I could sneak over and watch that....

A flash of movement barely caught my eye from down the street. By the time I had looked in that direction it was gone, but I was pretty sure it had been a person. Had they been wearing a uniform like mine? I squinted in the haze, and realized that there was another set of doors down at that end of the building.

I started that way, walking fast. I passed the other doors and saw that one of them was slightly ajar, as if someone had closed it gently so that it paused just before locking. I hurried to the corner—

There was Penny! It was the version of her from the cave, in a colonial jumpsuit like me. She was moving up the block quickly, with an excited bounce in her step, swinging her arms around, and I couldn't hear her, but I was sure she was singing to herself. She was probably so amazed to be back on Earth, with no idea the trouble she was about to cause.

I almost called out to her, but instead walked fast to catch up. She was passing right in front of the schools—man, did she have any idea how much of a risk she was taking?—but luck was with her, at least for a few more minutes, because no one seemed to notice either of us.

We reached the block between school and the market, a good place to get her attention, but there was an older woman walking her dog on the other side of the street. I focused on catching up. Getting closer, I figured I'd reach her while she waited at the intersection.

But the traffic lights changed just as she got there, and Penny strode right out into the crosswalk. The market was on the other side.

The walk light began to flash. I broke into a jog,

reached the street, and was halfway across when the light changed and the cars on either side began to move. I had to stop on the narrow median, watching helplessly as Penny pulled open the door to the market.

No! These were the most important minutes in the universe! I wiped the sweat out of my eyes and watched the cars humming by, and when a gap appeared I dashed across. A horn beeped but I made it and rushed up the sidewalk, then slowed as I neared the door, and cautiously pulled it open.

Maleen, the owner, wasn't at the counter. There was Penny, standing near the display of candy, frowning at her communicator. She glanced around.... This was the moment. She'd realized she couldn't pay for anything. Now she crouched down beside the display and reached out—

"Penny!" My hand fell on top of hers just as she was picking up the first package of Cocoa Pandas.

"Hey, what—" She flinched and pulled her hand

back, and then she looked up at me and her eyes bugged. "Will?" A glance at my clothes. "Wait are you…my Will? Like, from the cave?"

"Yeah! Listen, Penny, this is really serious: You can't take that candy."

Penny looked side to side and got that half smile like she did when she was about to deny something. "What are you talking about?"

"I know you're going to steal it."

"I wasn't—wait, how could you even know that?"

"Because you just realized that your credits wouldn't work and that Maleen was in the back room and would never notice. You're going to tell me this when you come back to the cave."

"Okay…but if *you're* telling me this, does that mean that you're, like…a future you? From *after* I do this?"

"Yeah. There's more to it than that, though—"

Penny threw up her hands. "But if I come back to

the cave with the candy, then that means this works. So what's the problem?"

"The problem is *after* that. You—"

There was a rustling, and now Maleen returned, making his way behind the deli counter and toward the front of the store. He eyed us suspiciously. "Need any help?" he said.

"Nope, we're good, thanks!" Penny said with a smile. Then quietly to me: "Way to go and ruin that. I was really looking forward to some Green Tea Drops." She grabbed my arm and pulled me into another aisle. "I don't get it," she hissed. "Why'd you come back here to stop me if it works?"

"Because it doesn't work! I mean, it does...but only for, like, a minute. We barely got to eat any candy before you disappeared."

"Disappeared? What's that supposed to mean?"

"I came here from another future, an alternate timeline—"

Penny squinted at me. "Okay, speak non-nerd."

"Stealing the candy changes the entire future," I said, pointing to the ceiling. "Cameras, Penny. You forgot about them, and they caught you shoplifting, only they blamed the *old* you, the one that's here in the past, and she—I mean, you—got kicked off the mission. You and Dad ended up staying behind on Earth, and so you weren't with us when we crashed, and..."

Penny's face got pale. "Hold on. Should I feel like my brain is about to explode, because..." She motioned with her hands blowing away from her head. "How can I not be with you in the future if I'm standing here now? I was literally just with you."

"It's, like, time travel stuff," I said. "It's what Judy was warning us about—"

"Oh man, she must be so mad at me."

"Actually, she doesn't really remember it even happened."

"Oh," said Penny. "There's some upside."

"Not really. Stealing the candy messes everything up, and that's why I'm here."

"Okay, but so…doesn't that mean we're good now?" Penny pointed to the candy rack. "You just stopped me, so this future I supposedly created isn't going to happen. Right?"

"I think so."

"You think so?"

"I can't be sure until we get back."

Penny looked around. "You can probably imagine how weird this sounds, considering that I don't remember any of what you're talking about."

"Believe me, it's even weirder when you do." I tugged her arm. "We need to get back to school and go through the doorway before anything else can go wrong."

"I thought you said you came from another future, though," said Penny, her brow furrowing.

"Yeah, I did, but we can't go that way. That door is gone."

"But if we go through mine, isn't, like, the *old* you going to be sitting there, waiting for me to come back?"

"Well…" I hadn't thought about that. Penny was right. The old me was in the cave with Judy. But *this* me was from a future created by the candy stealing. And now the candy hadn't been stolen. So what did that mean? Were we really two people? What exactly was going to happen to *this* me? I patted myself on the chest, like to make sure I was still all there.

"You thinking about that old movie where the kid has to get his parents to meet or he'll disappear?" said Penny.

"I don't know." My voice came out hoarse.

Penny patted my arm. "Relax, little brother. It will probably be fine. So says the girl who nearly changed the course of history." She smiled and put her arm around me and led me toward the door. "So long, Maleen," she said, waving to the counter. "Feel free to forget we were ever here." He looked at us with a confused expression as we left.

Outside, the sun had really started to heat up the haze—it could never really burn all the way through it—and the air felt heavy and electric.

"Wow," Penny said, "so I almost messed things up big time, huh?"

"You sound like you're proud."

"I mean"—Penny shrugged—"it's just, that's some powerful stuff, you know? Usually I have to defend why anything I do matters, but this…"

"It kinda made me and Mom and Judy probably die on the planet. It all goes worse without you and Dad there."

Penny's face fell. "Yikes."

We crossed the street and I caught a hot gust of bus exhaust and coughed, feeling that old itch intensify in my lungs.

"Do you know why I did it?" said Penny.

"What, steal the candy? Because you thought you'd get away with it?"

"Well, duh, but I like to think shoplifting isn't my normal gig. The real reason was—and I'm not supposed to tell you this—I overheard Mom and Dad talking the other morning, about the planet…" She looked at the ground. "There's something wrong with the sun—"

"A black hole," I finished. "It's affecting the orbit, and the planet's surface is going to burn."

"Yeah, how did you know about that?"

"In the other future, Mom told the whole group. And she said that because we lost our *Jupiter* in the ice—"

"Wait, what? The *Jupiter* is gone?"

"In the *other* future. It should still be there when we get back, now."

"Okay, sorry. My bad."

"So then Victor tried to take off, and their ship exploded, and it was all a huge mess."

"Exploded?" Penny's eyes went wide. "Like, they died?"

"They should be fine now, too. I mean, I'm pretty sure."

Penny shook her head. "Man, I was feeling so scared about that black hole stuff and I'd been wanting to tell you guys, but I knew Mom didn't want anyone to know yet. I guess carrying that secret was gnawing at me and made me reckless. I was like, *What's a little stolen candy when we all might die on some far-off planet?*"

"Well, hopefully now our chances are better," I said. "The candy was really good, though."

"I can't believe I didn't even get to try any."

We crossed in front of the schools. I kept my eyes peeled, but we were lucky, again, and rounded the corner to the auditorium doors.

"Wait, stop." Penny tugged on my sleeve.

"We have to get back—"

"I know, but take a moment." She put her arms

out and turned her face to the sky. "This is our last chance…which is funny because when we left here I thought *that* was our last chance, and now here we are, but…" She breathed in deep. "Ahh, Earth." Her nose wrinkled. "Man, docs it smell."

I smiled and looked around, feeling that old tightness in my throat, but this time it was more than just the bad air. Penny was right: It did smell, and the dust was toxic, and the food supply was unstable, and there wasn't enough space…but it had still been home. And it spun my head to think of how that other me in school right now, all excited about his Trash Bot, had *no* idea what was to come. No idea that his worst fear—of something happening to the *Resolute*, of being lost in space—would actually become a reality.…

"Are you sure we shouldn't tell somebody?" said Penny, like she was thinking the same thing. "Even just, like, leave Mom a note or something? I was thinking on my walk over here: If they knew about the attack on the *Resolute*, maybe they could be ready. Maybe we'd never have to crash and be lost in the first place."

"I don't know." It seemed like an obvious thing to do. Except I thought of what Hiroki had said about ripples affecting more ripples. "Any change we make is going to lead to new unknowns, and we have no idea how many. At least, the way things are now, we're alive and together. I don't think we can risk messing that up again."

Penny nodded. "True, and explaining that we got here via an alien time portal would be pretty tricky." Her face fell, and I saw tears welling up. "Did you miss me when I was left behind?"

Suddenly, I threw my arms around her. "A lot."

She hugged me back, both of us sweaty on the too-hot planet. "Okay, let's go home, then."

Hearing that almost made me laugh, thinking that *there* might really be home instead of here.

I pulled away and turned toward the auditorium. I wiped the tears out of my eyes, as they were making my vision blurry—

Except then the blur moved.

"What?" Penny said when I flinched against her.

It could have been the heat off the road, but I knew better. I grabbed Penny's arm. "Come on!" I spun around, yanking her in the other direction—

And slammed right into something solid. A flash of sparks, and there was a tall, hooded figure, its goggles glowing bright red.

Penny screamed, and they had her, too, had both of us in their powerful grips. They spun us around and there in the middle of the sidewalk was a doorway, eerie green dark glowing on the other side. The aliens shoved us forward and across the galaxy.

CHAPTER

15

I rushed through blazing white light, and it felt like I was traveling so much farther than I had before, as if I were being stretched out across all reality. My vision and my thoughts getting fuzzy and my body feeling so, so cold—

And then I was on the other side and falling to the ground in murky darkness. I stayed there for a second, on my hands and knees, flexing my fingers against the floor. It was smooth and warm. At first I thought it was metal, but it had a sheen to it more like mica, as if it were made of crystal.

Penny was beside me, on her hands and knees, too. Three of those alien beings were stepping around from behind us, no longer invisible, their cloaks brushing on the ground. They approached two others who stood at a console in front of us: a black pedestal that looked like it was made of a spiraling mass of black and red wires, with overlapping holographic screens fanning out from the top.

Over by the wall, I saw the Robot. He was wrapped in thick metal bonds, like enormous handcuffs that encircled his entire body. His face lights seemed like they'd been paused in place. *Hey!* I thought, hoping he would hear me, but he didn't respond.

There was a greenish glow coming from behind us. The doorway that we had come through was just one in a line of many that curved out of sight, like we were on the outside of a large circle of them, each one showing a view of stars.

Past that, across the room, was a circular wall that curved back around behind the alien beings. It was striped with black panels made of the same stuff as this floor, and in between were huge windows that—whoa.

At first, I didn't even understand what I was seeing. Through those windows, I saw huge rings of metal, and it took me a second to realize those were part of this ship that we were on, fanning out around us, sort of like the structure of the *Resolute*, but so much bigger. I could see at least five or six rings, and each one was massively thick, striped with hundreds of rows of windows. And beyond that was an enormous planet. Not the planet we were stranded on, but another completely different one that looked like it might be ten times bigger than Earth, based on the moons that I could see here and there. It was dimly lit in a strange way that I didn't quite understand, a sort of foggy haze of blue and gray clouds.

Beyond the planet was a feathery green-and-purple nebula, and then I realized something about the strange light on the planet: It wasn't the light of a star—like, with one side brightly lit and the other in a deep shadow. This whole planet seemed to be lit evenly, and then I understood that the light was coming from all those other floating objects: They weren't actually moons at all.

They were other huge ships like this one.

Each one had a massive blue engine firing out of the top and bottom of its core. It was the light from all these ships that was making the planet glow. And there were little lights darting between them, other smaller ships, and I mean, like, *thousands*.

Looking around, I realized that there was no star—Wait, there was one, but it was incredibly small, and at first I had mistaken it for another, distant ship. It was whitish blue and barely glimmering. I guessed it was a white dwarf: the dying gasp of a star that used to be like our sun.

"Will," Penny whispered beside me. "Where are we?"

"I think it's their home."

"Okay…but *where* is it? And who are they?"

Cold fear surged through me. "I have no idea."

The beings were talking to one another, their voices like reedy whispers punctuated now and then by clicking sounds.

One of them stepped away and came toward us. Like the others, its face was hidden in a hood, and we could see only those red-glowing goggles. I stood up, and so did Penny. As the being stopped in front of us, Penny took my hand.

Its goggles flickered and it began to speak in its windy, clicky language. I had no idea what it was saying, but after a second the words started to translate and we could understand them.

"You are right," the being said, its words like sharp-edged whispers. "This is our home. Generations ago, we faced disaster on the surface of our planet, and so we harnessed the energy of our star and used it to build this network across the galaxy. A network that you made unauthorized use of and nearly damaged."

"*Unauthorized?*" Penny snapped. "You guys left a doorway in a cave on our planet! And it turned on without us doing anything."

The being made a sharp inhaling sound. "That is not your planet. You are not even supposed to be there."

"Believe me," said Penny, "we don't want to be."

"We're sorry," I said. "We didn't mean to mess anything up. But my sister is right; we found the doorway by accident, and then it just opened up for me when I touched it. And when it showed us our old home, we just really wanted to go there again."

"You know that planet your doorway is on is going to, like, melt pretty soon, right?" said Penny.

"Of course we do," said the alien. "That is precisely why we use it for disposal."

"Disposal?" said Penny.

"Those battery things," I said. "The ones we saw in that pit."

"Expended antimatter cells," said the being. "They are vital to making this technology possible, but they are also highly unstable. We bring them to that planet to be incinerated, knowing they will cause no harm to any intelligent life."

"Thanks a lot," said Penny. "So that planet we're on is basically your garbage dump?"

The being made a sound like a sigh and didn't respond.

I looked again at the curling line of doorways behind us. "How many parts of the universe can you go to?"

"We have mapped six hundred and seventy-five billion light-years of the galactic. So, only a small portion."

"Wow," I said.

Penny flashed a glance at me and I saw her take a

deep breath. "I guess, then, compared to what you guys have seen, maybe we don't really rate as intelligent life." She cocked her thumb at the doorway behind us. "Probably makes the most sense to just let us go back to where we came from. No harm, no foul, right?"

"Yeah," I said, "and we'll make sure that we leave that door alone. Hopefully, we'll be off that planet soon anyway, and then it will all be fine."

The being turned toward its counterparts. They whispered in their own language, and the being turned back to us. "While it is true that you are, by most accounts, insignificant, it is also true that in just your brief interaction with our technology, you have managed to cause numerous space-time inconsistencies that have threatened the dimensional integrity not only of our transit system, but also of the universe itself. As your friend put it, timeline changes spread like ripples, and the work of restoring prime causality is painstaking and dangerous, not only for us, but for every living thing in the universe."

"You heard me talking to Hiroki?" I said. "So you *are* reading my mind?"

"We have had access to your brainwaves since you interacted with the doorway—a right you would have known you'd granted us, by the way, if you'd read the user agreement before accessing our system, as you are technically required to do."

"Sorry, we didn't see any paperwork lying around in your spooky cave," said Penny.

"It is clearly posted on the wall, but that is beside the point. We have been monitoring your actions to determine whether or not we need to intervene. Your mechanized assistant made that significantly more complicated." The being motioned to the Robot, who still just stood there vacantly.

"Okay, well," I said, "we're really sorry about this. What if we promise from now on that we won't use the doorway at all? And that we won't tell anyone about it." The being just stared at me. "I could have my Robot guard the cave entrance. Nobody can get past him."

"Except for you."

"But I swear that I wouldn't!"

The alien crossed its arms. "We are sympathetic to your situation, but what you are saying only proves our point. Life-forms like yourselves have far too much interconnection between your thoughts and your feelings. It is almost as if you can't tell the two apart. We have been running analysis on your brain function since the moment each of you first interacted with the doorway, and we have determined, with high confidence, that no matter what you say right now, you cannot be trusted with access to this kind of technology. It is simply too powerful for you to resist. You will turn to it again. And you *will* cause more damage. It is the way of your species."

"Why does it sound like you're not going to let us go home?" said Penny.

"We do feel that it was somewhat our error to allow you to engage with the system to begin with. We were not monitoring that planet for new life-forms, partly because of its remote location, but also because it seemed illogical that anyone would want to go there."

"We didn't want to go there," I said. "We crashed."

"Indeed... Therefore, we are willing to offer you a compromise. You two can stay here with us. We have a menagerie of curious species from around the universe, with simulated natural habitats that we feel are quite authentic. We could set up a similar one for you, as a courtesy. Perhaps based on your home planet."

"That sounds like a zoo," said Penny.

The being looked to its partners. They nodded. "As our guest, we would study you and add knowledge of your species to the great log of this universe."

"No! We can't stay here!" I said. "We have lives and families! Please let us go back. They won't know what happened to us!"

The being held out its hands. "I understand that this feels like a significant concern for you. We recognize how hard it is to be so attached to your emotions and you have our sympathies. But given the danger you pose, it's either stay here, or we can dispose of you. Those are your options."

Dispose...I couldn't get any words out. Had to think!

"Please let us go," said Penny, her eyes welling up.

"Please," I echoed, my eyes doing the same. I looked at the Robot again. *Help us*, I thought. He was still staring ahead, but just then his lights had started to flow toward the center. If that meant what I thought it meant...There was only one way to find out. I set my jaw and said, "Let us go, or else."

The being cocked its head at me. Penny looked at me, too. "Excuse me?"

I clenched my fists to try to keep from shaking. "Let us go or else."

"It is useless to speak in such a way," said the being. "You are no threat to us here."

"You're right, I'm not," I said. "But he is." And then I thought as hard as I could: *Save us now!*

"Will, what are you doing?" Penny hissed.

Be...bad.

The Robot's face lights swirled into a spiral pattern, and then all at once, they changed to red. By the time the beings had turned toward him, the plates up and down his body had begun to ripple and shift. The metal bonds around him warped and cracked, and then split. His two legs became four, and his human-shaped hands uncoiled into spiraling blades.

"Um, Will?" said Penny.

"Trust me," I said.

The being closest to us turned to the others and hissed urgently in their language. A shrill tone began to sound through the ship, like an alarm, and the beings rushed toward the Robot. Bursts of fire erupted from his blade hands, smashing into two of the beings and sending them flying across the room.

"Undo this programming!" the being shouted at me.

"Sorry!" I said, grabbing Penny's hand and backing toward the portal. "He's connected to me. Guess our feelings are a bit more significant than you thought."

"You can't—" the being began, but then the Robot shoved him and sent him crashing into the console. The holographic screens sizzled and winked out as the console crashed over, its wires sparking. The other beings ran from the room as the Robot spun, looking for more.

"We need to go now!" I called to him. "Change back!"

The Robot turned toward me, and for just a moment, his fiery face filled me with fear—What if he didn't remember me? What if he didn't change back?

But then he began to morph, his face cooling to blue, his plates rearranging themselves back to his humanlike form.

"Come on," I said to Penny. She was still staring at the Robot. I tugged her arm.

"Little brother," she said, shaking her head, "that is still completely freaky."

Bright flashes lit up the room and more aliens began to appear, their red-goggle eyes glowing. Unlike the ones in the robes, these figures wore black jumpsuits and were carrying large blasters that glowed with green circuitry.

"Hurry!" I shouted.

We turned back to the doorway, and I reached toward the starry view, pausing with my fingers centimeters away.

"What are you waiting for?" said Penny as the beings closed in.

"I just want to make sure I'm thinking about the moment in the cave, when you left, in the right timeline. We only get one shot at this."

"No kidding! Let's go!"

The Robot ran over and stood with his back to us, facing the approaching figures. He looked at me over his shoulder, and for a moment his face flashed red again, almost as if he was asking me, *Should I fight these guys, too?*

"It's okay, we're going back…." I focused on the memory of the cave with all of us there and moved my hand forward—

The Robot caught my wrist just before I touched the doorway. "What?" I said, spinning to him.

His lights were making the spiraling shape. "Danger," he said.

I saw that there were nearly a dozen aliens and they were closing cautiously from all sides, weapons raised. "We gotta go!"

But the Robot kept hold, and with his free hand,

reached and touched his own silver finger to the doorway. As the view of space started to whirl and spiral, he let go of my wrist and grasped the metallic frame of the door. There was a flash of green light, and the Robot's fingers began to separate in a way I'd never seen before. The metal plates spread apart, and little wires snaked out and wormed their way around and between the glowing circuitry of the doorway. The thin green tubes began to pulse, glowing brighter and brighter. A humming sound grew all around us. The entire door began to shake and glow.

"Will?" said Penny over the cycling sound.

"What are you doing?" I shouted to the Robot.

The sound was becoming deafening, and wind seemed to be coming from every direction, wrapping around us.

"Whatever it is, do it fast!" Penny looked fearfully over her shoulder.

The view zoomed in on the planet we'd crashed

on, down into the trees, into a dark space—was it the cave?—but at the same time, light was pouring out of the doorway, brighter and brighter, like the entire thing was being washed out.

Except it wasn't just the doorway; it was me, too. Everything I could see or think or feel. All of it fading away, as if I was losing touch with the world. The last thing I saw was the Robot grabbing my arm and pulling me through the doorway, into the light.

CHAPTER

16

For a moment there was nothing at all. I felt lost, as if I didn't even have a body. Like my thoughts were a collection of those fireflies we'd seen once at the bio preserve on Earth, darting and scattering and blinking faintly.

And then I found myself on my hands and knees again. This time, I thought for sure I was going to throw up. My guts hitched and I was barely able to hold it down. My head was splitting with pain, my whole body tingling like I'd been shocked with a loose wire. I shivered all over with this feeling like I had just been…what?

Gone. That was what it felt like. As if I hadn't even *been* for a moment. I know that sounds crazy, but I don't know any other way to describe it.

"Where are we?" I said in almost a whisper, but as my vision cleared I saw that we were in the cave. There was a light ahead, and when I squinted I saw the opening to the outside. Sunlight, trees, and then something large moving. One of the moth-asaurs, pacing on the far side of the pit.

Right, I thought, *the cave*. My brain was still moving slowly, my thoughts bubbling up like tar. *Wait, what about*—I spun around, but there was nothing behind us except for that tunnel descending into darkness, and that faint green light.

What had I been expecting? Aliens; a strange, giant ship…But all of it was so foggy. At least

I knew where I was right now. "*When* is this?" I asked, getting to my feet.

The Robot tapped my shoulder. I turned to see him holding a stick out to me. He motioned with his head, and I saw the crisscrossing lines drawn in the dirt.

The tic-tac-toe board. Yes! We were back where we were supposed to be! Except where was Penny, and Judy for that matter?

The Robot motioned to me with the stick again.

"Okay, okay," I said. I blinked hard, took the stick, and drew an O in the top right.

The Robot took the stick back, made an X in the bottom center, and then connected the vertical line of three that he'd made.

"Wow, you win," I said, shaking my head. "To be fair, I didn't really know what was going on."

One of the mothasaurs roared outside. I squinted at them, my thoughts still tumbling slowly like heavy boulders, and then I got it: "You brought us back to before, didn't you?" I glanced down the tunnel toward the green light. "We haven't gone down there yet. This is before all of it." But then I realized that all the memories were still there in my head: going to my old room, Penny using the doorway, the timeline without her and Dad, going back to get her and then ending up on that alien spaceship. All that had happened, I felt sure of it, except now it actually hadn't?

"Shouldn't there be, like, two of me here right now?" I said. Then I remembered how the Robot had not only touched the doorway, but his circuitry had intertwined with it. "Or is this something your super-advanced alien technology took care of, too?"

The Robot bent and erased our game, and drew a new grid.

I looked behind us, at that light. . . .

"Danger."

I nodded. "You brought us back to this moment so we won't do it at all," I said. "If we never use the doorway the first time, none of the bad stuff happens. The future doesn't change and the aliens never catch us. Everything is back to normal. No ripples in the pond at all."

The Robot's lights flowed faster.

A big feeling rushed through me. At first I thought it was relief, but then I realized it was also maybe sadness. "If we don't ever use the doorway, I can't see home one last time."

The Robot tapped my pocket, and I realized there was something in there. My thoughts were still jumbled and I was drawing a blank, but then my fingers curled around Captain Quasar.

I looked at the little figure and smiled. "I'll still have the memories and my videos." And something else occurred to me as I looked at the action figure: "Wait, am I the reason I couldn't find him when I was packing up? Is this how he got lost? Future me took him?"

The Robot didn't answer and instead held out

the stick. We played another game to a tie, and then the Robot started out of the cave.

"Hey, wait," I said, "the mothasaurs—"

The Robot strode right toward them, stopping at the pit where the aliens' antimatter cells were stored. Picturing their red-goggle eyes again gave me a chill, and I scanned the trees looking for any blurry shapes, but whatever the Robot had done to the portal must have bought us some time. Or maybe now that the future where we used the door wasn't going to happen, they would leave us alone. Or the Robot had scared them. He had that effect on people.

And mothasaurs. While they roared at the Robot, they stayed on the other side of the pit. I noticed that one still had that fresh wound in its side.

The Robot crouched and hauled up the first of the cells, its middle glowing hot white.

"Careful of the radiation," I said, standing aside as he walked by with the long cylinder over his shoulder. I could still feel the stinging of those burns on my arms and neck.

The Robot carried the cell into the cave and dropped it with a thud. Then he went and got the next one, and the next, until he had piled them all inside the tunnel entrance.

"Now what?" I said.

He moved to the cliffside of crumbled rock and picked up a large boulder.

"You're going to block it?"

"Danger." He carried the boulder over and dropped it in front of the entrance.

"Do you think that will keep those aliens from coming back?"

He picked up another boulder and added it to the pile. It smashed against the side of the entrance, causing more rocks to collapse from above.

"We can't keep them out if they want to come back," I said. "This is more to keep us from being tempted by the doorway again. So maybe they won't need to come back."

The Robot broke another boulder free, and then another. I watched the entrance to the tunnel close, rock by rock, and I nearly shouted at him to stop. This reality, where Dad and Penny were here and we still had our *Jupiter* was way better than the alternate one, but we were still in danger. What if that doorway really was our best chance of saving ourselves?

Except those alien beings had made it pretty clear they weren't going to allow that.

The Robot's next boulder caused a massive collapse from above. I waved rock dust away from my face and saw that the entrance was completely sealed. "That's it, then," I said.

The Robot turned to face me, his lights calm and flowing into the center.

"I know," I said. "It's just hard. You don't know what it's like to have feelings like this."

Except… "Maybe you do." When the Robot had

interfaced with the doorway, he could have taken us back to any moment from this past, especially one where we weren't in danger from these moth-asaurs, and yet he'd chosen the moment when we'd been playing tic-tac-toe. I wondered if, for him, that was a moment that he wanted to relive one more time, too, before it was gone.

Speaking of which: I looked at the giant crea-tures snarling at us from beyond the pit. With those cells gone, they were starting to edge around toward us. "What do we do about these guys?"

"Will!" A voice echoed from the forest. Mom! And now another: "Will!" It was Dad!

"Over here!" I shouted.

Penny burst into the clearing, followed by Judy, and then Mom and Dad.

The mothasaurs roared and spun toward them.

Dad stepped in front of them and leveled a flare gun. "Shield your eyes!" He fired and the flare slammed into the ground right between the mothasaurs, skidding between their feet in a fiery shower of sparks. The creatures shrieked and darted into the trees.

"Will!" Penny ran to me and put her hands on my shoulders. Her face was red, her hair wild around her face. "Are you all right?"

"Yeah," I said, "totally fine. I, um…are you?"

"I think so." She lowered her voice. "Do you remember…?"

"All of it," I said.

Penny looked relieved. "Good, because for a minute there I thought I was going a wee bit crazy. So, it happened."

"Yeah." I motioned to the blocked-up cave. "But now it's not going to. We should be okay."

Penny sighed. "Good."

"Hey, Will," Dad said, coming up beside her, and all at once I was overwhelmed by this feeling, almost like panic—

I threw myself at him and hugged him tight.

"Whoa," he said, putting his arms around me and patting my back. "It's okay, kiddo. You're safe now. It's all right."

"What's up with you guys?" said Judy, eyeing me as she approached. "Penny did the same thing to Mom when they got back."

"Yeah, what did we do to deserve all this affection?" said Mom.

"It's nothing," I said, pulling away and brushing at my eyes. "Just glad to see you guys, that's all." I made sure to hug Mom, too.

Dad shrugged. "Penny called us back to camp, said it was an emergency and we had to find you." He looked over my shoulder, and then around the clearing. "She was convinced you were in some kind of danger. Was it just those mothasaurs? Or was there something else?"

I eyed Penny. "Just them," I said. "But they seemed really hungry."

"What's up with this pit?" said Judy, peering into it. "It almost looks like someone dug it."

I watched her for a second, wondering if she'd have a flash of recognition, but she didn't seem to. "I don't know," I said. "I was thinking maybe it's a mothasaur nest or something."

"One of them looked injured," said Mom. She eyed the Robot. "Did he do that?"

No, time-traveling alien beings did. The words almost came out, but instead I shook my head. "I don't know. They were already hurt when we ran into them."

"Could be some other predator out here that we haven't seen yet," said Dad. "We should get back. And Will, I want you to stick a little closer to the *Jupiter* while we're gone from now on."

"Got it. Sorry. Hey, Mom, um, Victor and his family…"

"What did they do now?"

"Nothing, just...Are they all right?"

"Not the words I'd use to describe Victor," Dad muttered.

"As far as I know," said Mom, peering at me. "Why?"

"Nothing."

"Okay..." Mom didn't seem satisfied, but luckily she let it go, at least for the moment. As I now knew, she had a lot on her mind.

Mom and Dad turned and started back on the trail. Judy followed them, and Penny came over beside me. "Hey," she said, glancing over her shoulder. "Do you think we're safe? From those goggle-eyed dudes?"

"Maybe. I mean, they've got no reason to bother with us"—I made finger quotes—"*insignificant beings* now."

As I said that, though, I was actually thinking the opposite: I didn't think we'd seen the last of them. And it turned out I was right, but that's a story for another time.

Penny rolled her eyes. "I can't believe we almost ended up in a cosmic zoo. And I can't believe we can't tell anyone!" She pointed ahead. "Judy doesn't seem to have any idea."

"She never actually went through the doorway," I said.

"What does that say about us?" said Penny. "Do we have, like, weird time-travel brains now? Or—"

I grabbed her arm and held my finger to my lips, while motioning to Judy with my eyes.

She was singing something to herself. We both sped up until we were just behind her, and we heard:

"*Cocoa pandas in a tree...*"

Penny looked at me with wide eyes.

"Hey," I said to Judy. "How did that song get in your head?"

Judy whipped around, embarrassment flashing across her face. "I don't know. It was just on my mind today. They were my favorite candy back on

Earth. Sometimes I can still taste them.... Why are you two looking at me like that?"

"Nothing," I said. "Never mind."

"Okay, then." Judy shook her head and quickened her step to catch up with Mom and Dad.

We crossed the log bridge and followed the trail back to the lake. When we reached the grove of clapping flowers, the Robot slammed his hands together and the plants bloomed around us, making their magenta carpet. I smiled, but then my smile faded for just a moment. I paused and looked along the lakeside to the south.

"Hey." Penny turned back to me. "More weird memories?"

"It was really dangerous," I said. "The version when you weren't here."

"I am always saying that my importance on this mission is critically undervalued," she said with a smile.

"That thing you know about," I said. "That Mom hasn't told anyone yet."

Penny's smile faded. "I think she's going to tell the group later today."

"Don't worry," I said. "It's going to be all right."

"Well, I'm not so sure about that," said Penny, her face falling. "Unless you know something I don't?"

"Just that it could be worse," I said. "As long as we're all together, we've got our best chance."

Penny's eyes brimmed with tears, but then she rolled them and gave me a gentle shove. "Dork," she said, and headed up the trail.

My eyes felt hot, too. I wiped them and breathed deep. Then I turned to the Robot, who was waiting behind me, his blue lights shooting in toward the center. "Race you back to camp!"

I took off up the trail with the Robot's big, heavy steps pounding behind me and a grin on my face.

Acknowledgments

It's been a thrill to hang out with Will Robinson and the gang in the Lost in Space universe, and for that, I first want to thank my amazing editor Mary-Kate Gaudet, who helped this story soar while solving various space-time conundrums, both fictional and real, along the way. Thanks to Regan Winter and the team at Little, Brown for putting so much effort and energy into this book. Thanks to Derek Thielges and everyone at Synthesis Entertainment as well as Legendary for letting me play in their amazing world. Thanks as ever to my outstanding agent, Robert Guinsler, for his guidance and support, and the rest of the team at Sterling Lord Literistic. Thanks to my readers, to the teachers, librarians, and booksellers who have supported my books. And finally, special thanks to my family, friends, and my very own *Jupiter* crew: Annie, Willow, and Elliott. I couldn't travel the stars without you.